"It's rude grumbled

"Honey," Jordan said, "the whole point of that get-up you're wearing is to make men stare. Besides, I came to watch you dance."

"You," she growled, "came to watch everyone else watch me dance, and to make sure no one did anything improper like *speak* to me."

Jordan took a step forward. "Are you telling me you *want* to converse with these yahoos?"

"I'm telling you it's none of your business what I do!"

His voice as soft as melted butter, Jordan whispered, "I want it to be my business. Keeping my hands off you has been hell, Georgia."

Her heart slammed into her ribs. He reached for her, touched her face with a gentleness she'd never known, and her knees went weak. "Jordan?"

Even to her own ears his name sounded like a plea. The past few weeks had been rough for her, too. The memory of his touch haunted her, and her nightly dreams were getting hotter and hotter....

Dear Reader,

After four books, the Buckhorn brothers have become like close friends to me. I'm proud of these men, and I like them very much. I hope you do, too.

Jordan's story was written last for personal reasons. I live by priorities, and for me, children (my own especially, but all children really) have to be a priority. Love them unconditionally, but provide them with the boundaries they need and want. Give the best direction you can, then let them stand on their own two feet. Accept them as individuals. Show them strength and kindness—and insist they show it, too.

And whenever possible, find a wonderful man like one of the Buckhorn brothers to love you, accept you and emotionally support you. Then return all the same to him.

I'm happy to report that readers who have been asking for Annie's story, and for Max's, will get their wish. Look for my special double Duets #47 in March 2001 featuring *Annie, Get Your Guy* and *Messing Around with Max*. Then in July 2001, my first Harlequin single title, *Caught in the Act*, will be in bookstores!

My best to all of you,

Lori Foster
(Lorifoster@poboxes.com;http//www.eclectics.com/lorifoster)

THE BUCKHORN BROTHERS

Lori Foster
JORDAN

HARLEQUIN®

TORONTO • NEW YORK • LONDON
AMSTERDAM • PARIS • SYDNEY • HAMBURG
STOCKHOLM • ATHENS • TOKYO • MILAN • MADRID
PRAGUE • WARSAW • BUDAPEST • AUCKLAND

To my husband, Allen
Thank you for giving me so much: unconditional love,
endless support, the closest of friendships and three
wonderful sons who are so much like you!
There's nothing more I need, nothing more I really want.
Everything else is just icing on the cake.
Together, we have been very, very blessed.

Love you always, me.

ISBN 0-373-25898-4

JORDAN

Copyright © 2000 by Lori Foster.

Printed in U.S.A.

1

THE SWINE.

Jordan Sommerville stared at the hand-painted sign positioned crookedly over the ramshackle building. Visible from the roadway, the sign boasted some of the worst penmanship he'd ever seen. The bright red letters seemed to leap right out at him.

He cursed as another icy trickle of rain slid down the back of his neck. He could hear the others behind him, murmuring in subdued awe as they took in the sights and sounds of the bar. It was late, it was dark, and for September, it was unseasonably cool. Surely there didn't exist a more idiotic way to spend a Friday night.

The idea of trying to convince a bar owner to institute a drink limit, especially a bar owner who had thus far allowed quite a few men to overimbibe, seemed futile. Jordan started forward, anxious to get it over with.

Somehow he'd become the designated leader of the five-man troop, a dubious honor he'd regretfully accepted. The men had been organized by Zenny, a retired farmer who was best described as cantankerous—on his good days. Then there was Walt and Newton, who claimed to be semiretired from their small-town shops, though they still spent every day

there. And Howard and Jesse, the town gossips who
volunteered for every project, just to make sure they
got to stick their noses into anything that was going
on.

Jordan stopped at the neon-lighted doorway to the
seedy saloon and turned to face the men. A strobing
beer sign in the front window illuminated their rapt
faces. Jordan had to shout to be heard over the loud
music and laughter blaring from inside the establish-
ment.

"Now remember," he said, and though he used his
customary calm tone, he infused enough command to
hold all their attention, "we're going to *talk*. That's all.
There'll be no accusations, no threats and absolutely,
under no circumstances, will there be any violence.
Understood?"

Five heads bobbed in agreement even as they
looked anxiously beyond Jordan to the rambunctious
partying inside. Jordan sighed.

Buckhorn County was dry, which meant anyone
who drank had the good sense to stay indoors and
keep it private. There'd been too many accidents on
the lake, mostly from vacationers who thought water
sports and alcohol went hand in hand, for the citizens
to want it any other way.

But this new bar, a renovated old barn, had opened
just over the county line, so the same restriction didn't
apply. Lately, some of its customers had tried joyrid-
ing through Buckhorn in the dead of the night, hitting
fences, tearing up cornfields, terrorizing the farm animals, and generally making minor mayhem. No one
had been seriously injured, yet, but in the face of such
moronic amusements, it was only a matter of time.

So the good citizens of Buckhorn had rallied together and, at the suggestion of the Town Advisory Board, decided to try talking to the owner of the bar. They hoped he would be reasonable and agree to restrict drinks to the rowdier customers, or perhaps institute a drink limit for those that leaned toward nefarious tendencies and overindulgence.

Jordan already knew what a waste of time that would be. He had his own very personal reasons for loathing drunks. He would have gently refused to take part in the futile endeavor tonight, except that he and his brothers were considered leading citizens of Buckhorn, and right now, due to a nasty flu that had swept through the town, Jordan was the only brother available to lead.

With a sigh, he walked through the scarred wooden doors and stepped inside. The smoke immediately made his lungs hurt. Mixed with the smells of sweat and the sickening sweet odor of liquor, it was enough to cause the strongest stomach to lurch.

The dank, dark night worked as a seal, enclosing the bar in a sultry cocoon. The walls were covered with dull gray paint. Long fluorescent lights hung down from the exposed ceiling beams, adding a dim illumination to an otherwise gloomy scene.

Men piled up behind Jordan, looking over his shoulder, breathing on his neck, tsking at what they saw as salacious activity. Which didn't, of course, stop them from ogling the scene in deep fascination. Jordan could almost feel their anticipation and knew the evening was not destined to end well.

Hoping to locate someone in charge, Jordan looked around. A heavy, sloping counter seated several men, all of them hanging over their beers while a painfully skinny, balding man refilled drinks with the quickness of long practice. At the end of the bar stood a massive, menacing bouncer, the look on his face deliberately intimidating. Jordan snorted, seeing the ploy for what it was; a way to keep the peace in a place that cultivated disagreements by virtue of what it was and the purpose it served.

There were booths lining the walls and a few round tables cluttering up the middle of the floor. Overall, the place seemed crowded and loud, but not lively. An atmosphere of depression hung in the air despite the bawdy laughter.

Then suddenly the noise of conversation, clinking glasses and rowdy music died away. In its place a heavy, expectant hush filled the air. Jordan felt the hair on his arms tingle with a subtle awareness. Everyone stared at a low stage to the left of the front door, almost in the center of the bar. It couldn't have been more than eight feet wide and ten feet long. A faded, threadbare curtain at the back of the stage rustled but didn't open.

Jordan stared, feeling as mesmerized as everyone else, though he had no idea why. Behind him, old man Zenny coughed. Walt eased closer. Newton bumped into his left side.

Slowly, so slowly Jordan hardly noticed it at first, music from a hidden stereo began to filter into the quiet. It crackled a bit, as if the speakers had been subjected to excessive volume. It started out low and easy and gradually built to a rousing tempo that made him think of the *Lone Ranger* series. All the men who'd previously been loud were now subdued and waiting.

The curtain parted just as the music grabbed a bouncing beat and took off like a horse given his lead. Jordan caught his breath.

A woman, slight in build except for her truly exceptional breasts, burst onto the stage in what appeared to be an aerobic display except that she moved with the music...and looked seductive as hell.

He'd seen his three sisters-in-law do similar steps while exercising, but then, his sisters-in-law didn't have breasts like this woman, and they were always dressed in sweats when they worked out.

And they sure as certain didn't perform for drunks.

Nearly spellbound, Jordan couldn't pull his gaze away. His mouth opened on a deep breath, his hands curled into fists and his body tightened. The reaction surprised him and kept him off guard.

As he stared he realized the woman wasn't exactly doing a seductive dance. But the way she moved, fluid and graceful and fast, each turn or twist or high kick keeping time to the throbbing beat, had every man in the bar—including Jordan—holding his breath, balanced on a keen edge of anticipation.

She wore a revealing costume of black lace, strategically placed fringe, and little else. The fringe glittered with jet beads that moved as she moved, drawing attention to her bouncing breasts and rotating hips. Her legs were slender, sleekly muscled. She turned her back to the bar, and the fringe on her behind did a little *flip—flip—flip*. Jordan's right hand twitched, just imagining what that bottom would feel like.

He cursed under his breath. The costume covered her, and yet it didn't. He'd seen women at the lake wearing bikinis that were much more revealing, but none that were sexier. She kept perfect time with the heavy pulsing of the music and within two minutes her shoulders and upper chest gleamed with a fine mist of sweat, making her glow. Her full breasts, revealed almost to her nipples, somehow managed to stay inside her skimpy costume, but the thought that they might not kept Jordan rigid and enrapt.

Next to him, Newton whispered, "Lord have mercy," and the same awe Jordan felt was revealed in the older man's voice. Jordan scowled, wishing he could send the men back outside, wishing he could somehow cover the woman up.

He didn't want others looking at her. But he could have looked at her all night long.

His possessive urges toward a complete stranger were absurd, so he buried them away behind a dose of contempt while ignoring the punching beat of his heart.

The audience cheered, screamed, banged their thick beer mugs on the counter and on the tabletops. Yet the woman's expression never changed. She didn't smile, though her overly lush, wide mouth trembled slightly with her exertions. She had a mouth made for kissing, for devouring. Her lips looked soft and Jordan knew with a man's intuition exactly how sweet they'd feel against his own mouth, his skin. Every now and then she turned in such a way that the lighting reflected in her pale gray eyes, which stared straight ahead, never once focusing on any one man.

In fact, her complete and utter disregard for her all-male audience was somehow arousing. She looked to be the epitome of sexual temptation, but didn't care.

She might have been dancing alone, in the privacy of her bedroom, for all the attention she gave to the shouting, leering spectators.

Feigning nonchalance, Jordan crossed his arms over his chest and decided to wait until her show ended before finding the proprietor. Not because she interested him. Of course not. But because right now it would be useless to start his search, being that everyone was caught up in the show.

Despite his attempt at indifference, Jordan's gaze never left her, and every so often it seemed his heartbeat mirrored her rhythm. Beneath his skin, a strange warmth expanded, pulsed. Something about her, something elusive yet intrinsically female, called to him. He ignored the call. He was not a man drawn in by flagrant sexuality. No, when a woman caught his attention, it was because of her gentleness, her intelligence, her morals. Unlike his brothers—who were the finest men he knew—he'd never been a slave to his libido. They'd often teased him about his staid personality, his lack of fire, because he'd made a point of keeping his composure in all things. *At least most of the time.*

His eyes narrowed.

Short, golden brown curls framed her face and were beginning to darken with sweat, clinging to her temples and her throat. It was an earthy look, dredging up basic primal appetites. Jordan wondered what those damp curls would feel like in his fingers, what her heated skin would taste like to his tongue. How her warmed body would feel under his, moving as smoothly to his sexual demands as it moved to the music.

As the rhythmic beat began to fade, she dropped smoothly to her knees, then her stomach. Palms flat on the floor, arms extended, she arched her body in a parody of a woman in the throes of pleasure. The move was blatantly sexual, deliberately seducing, causing the crowd to almost riot and making Jordan catch his breath.

Her face was exquisite at that moment, eyes closed, mouth slightly parted, nostrils flaring. Jordan locked his jaw against the mental images filling his brain—images of him holding her hips while she rode him in just that way, taking him deep inside her body.

He wanted to banish the thoughts, but they wouldn't budge. Anger at himself and at the woman conflicted with his growing tension.

He knew every damn man in the place was imagining the same thing and it enraged him.

In that instant her eyes slowly opened and her glittering gray gaze locked on his. Jordan sucked in a breath, feeling as though she'd just touched him in all the right places. They were connected as surely as any lovers, despite the space between them, the surroundings and the lack of prior knowledge. Her eyes turned hot and a bit frightened as they filled with awareness.

Then she caught herself and with a lift of her chin, she swung her legs around and came effortlessly to her feet.

Scowling at the unexpected effect of her, Jordan tried, without success, to pull his gaze away. There was nothing about a mostly naked vamp dancing in a sleazy bar for the delectation of drunks that should appeal to him.

So why was he so aroused?

He hadn't had such a staggering reaction to a female since his teens when puberty had made him more interested in sex than just about anything else. But he'd grown up since then. He was a mature, responsible man now. He was...

The music died away to utter silence. The hush in the room was rich and hungry.

She wasn't beautiful, Jordan insisted to himself, attempting to argue away his racing heartbeat, his clenched muscles and his swelling sex. In fact, she was barely pretty. But she was as sexy as the original temptation, her appeal basic and erotic.

Over the silence, Jordan detected the sound of her heavy breathing with the force of a thunderclap. A roar of approval started the massive applause, and within seconds the room rocked with the sounds of masculine appreciation and entreaties for more. Jordan continued to watch her, not smiling, not about to encourage her. He waited for her to meet his gaze again, but she didn't. She looked straight ahead, deliberately ignoring him.

Anger simmered inside him, warring with lust.

Slowly, still struggling for breath, she took a bow. He hadn't noticed until that moment that she wore high heels. Amazing, he thought, remembering how she'd moved, the gracefulness of her every step. Her legs looked especially long in the spiked heels.

She tottered slightly as if in exhaustion, appearing young and vulnerable for the space of a heartbeat. Money was thrown onstage, some of it hitting the open urn positioned at the edge, most of it landing around her feet. She didn't bend to pick it up or acknowledge the money in any way. She merely stood there, as proud and imperious as a queen while the men payed homage, begging her for more, emptying their pockets.

If Jordan hadn't been watching her so closely, he wouldn't have seen her hands curl into fists, or the way her soft mouth tightened. With one last nod of her head, she turned to leave the stage. That's when the trouble started.

Two men reached for her, one catching her wrist, the other stroking her knee and thigh.

A wave of rage hit Jordan with such force, it nearly took him to his knees.

He couldn't dispute his own reaction, and started toward her. At almost the same time, the bouncer pushed himself away from the back wall, but Jordan barely noticed him. He kept his gaze on the woman's face as she tried to pull her hand free, but the drunken men had other plans. One of them attempted to press money into her hand while he suggested several lecherous possibilities, egged on by his buddy.

Others seconded the drunks' suggestions, throwing more money, making catcalls and urging her to another dance...and more.

She firmly refused, and again tried to step away. Her gaze sought out the bouncer, but he'd been detained by a table full of younger men who were insisting the woman should continue.

Jordan reached the edge of the stage just as she said, "Go on home to your wife, Larry. The show's over."

Her deep throaty voice was filled with loathing and exhaustion. It affected Jordan almost as strongly as the sight of the drunk's rough hand wrapped around her slender wrist. He barely restrained himself from attacking the man, and that alone was an aberration. Jordan had never considered himself a violent or overly aggressive person.

"Let the lady go."

Reacting to the command in Jordan's tone, the man released her automatically, only to turn on Jordan with a growl.

"Who the hell are you?" As he asked it, Larry took a threatening step forward.

Jordan gave him a stark look of contempt. In as reasonable a voice as he could muster, considering his mood and the obstreperous noise of the bar, he said, "You're drunk and I'm not. I'm bigger in every way. And right now, I'd like to tear you in two." Jordan watched him, his gaze unwavering. "Does it really matter who I am?"

Larry reeked of alcohol, as if he'd been at the bar all day. Perhaps that accounted for his loss of good sense. But for whatever reason, he disregarded Jordan's warning and attempted a clumsy punch. Jordan leaned back two inches so that Larry's limp fist whipped right past his jaw, then he stuck his foot out, gave the smaller man a shove, and sent him sprawling. Larry screeched like a wet hen, but when he hit the dusty barn floor he landed hard, and he didn't look sober enough to get back up.

"Oh, for heaven's sake..." The dancer's words were muttered low, but Jordan heard her. He glanced up. The other man stepped back quickly at the look of menace in Jordan's eyes. Unfortunately, he still had his hand hooked around the woman's knee and his sudden retreat pulled her off balance. With a loud gasp, she stumbled right off the edge of the low stage and would have landed next to Larry if Jordan hadn't caught her.

The impact of her small, lush body caused Jordan to stumble, too, but he easily regained his balance and, acting on pure male instinct, wrapped his arms tightly around her bottom. Her belly landed flush against his lower chest, her ripe breasts pressed to his face. Jordan stood, for a single instant, stunned.

Her small hands felt cool on his burning skin, the contrast maddening. Braced against his shoulders, she pushed back and Jordan was able to see her angry face.

"Are you *insane?*" she demanded.

"At this moment?" Jordan asked, unable to concentrate on anything of import, not with those incredible breasts a mere breath away. "I believe so."

He held very still, feeling trapped by her nearness, by the deep timbre of her voice, her warm, gentle weight, her seductive movements. Her body was lithe and supple, soft, despite her determination to push away from him. Acutely aware of one firm breast pressing into his jaw, he could see far too much cleavage to allow for divided attention.

Her black lace bodysuit dipped low in front, displaying the paleness and lush roundness of her breasts; the material was so sheer he could plainly make out the outline of her puckered nipples, thrusting noticeably against the material. His mouth went dry. He was so hard he hurt.

He wanted to taste her.

Contrary to all reason, to the situation, to the crowd around them, *to his own basic nature,* he wanted to draw her into the heat of his mouth, lick her, taste her, hear her husky moans. He'd only need to turn his head a scant two inches and...

His breath came faster, his stomach cramped.

Her naked thighs were sleek and smooth and warm against his forearms, which he had crossed beneath her bottom. Up close, her overdone makeup was even more apparent—but then, so was her allure. Jordan met her gaze and they each stalled.

Her pale skin was tinged pink from exertion and embarrassment. Her nose was narrow, tilted up on the end like an innocent pixie's, her mouth so full and soft he could almost feel the effect of it against his skin, making his body throb. Her face was a perfect oval, her cheeks a little too round, her chin a little too stubborn. But those arctic gray eyes...

He'd never seen any like them.

Her breath caught sharply as he studied her mouth. With a burst of near panic, she began her struggles anew. Her efforts to free herself from his hold set them off-kilter and Jordan fell back a step.

A rickety table overturned as he bumped into it, spilling several drinks. Jordan, feeling a little drunk himself as he breathed in the smell of her musky, heated skin, especially strong between her soft breasts, attempted to regain his balance and apologize at the same time.

He wasn't given a chance. This time the man swinging his meaty fist had better aim. Jordan quickly tried to set the dancer on her feet even as he ducked. He wasn't fast enough to do either.

His head snapped back from a solid clip in the jaw. Pain exploded, but Jordan didn't lose his hold on the woman. In fact, his arms felt locked, unable to open even when he wanted them to.

Ears ringing from the blow, Jordan allowed his anger to erupt. Because of how he held her, that fist had come entirely too close to touching a woman.

His head now clearer, Jordan gently released his feminine bundle and moved her behind his back, keeping her there when she attempted to stall the fight. He eyed the man who'd struck him, and with a sharp, lightning-fast reflex that was more automatic than not, Jordan used the backward sweep of his bent arm to slam his elbow into the man's jaw. His blow was far more powerful than the one he'd received, and the man sank like a brick in water. Other than his arm, Jordan hadn't moved—and his mood was deadly.

All hell broke loose.

The bouncer who'd just witnessed Jordan's retaliation came charging forward. Jordan sighed. He wasn't a regular, which he supposed meant he was automatically tagged as the troublemaker.

Looking quickly around for the older men who'd come with him, Jordan found them safely ensconced in the far corner near the front door where they could watch while staying unharmed. He didn't have time to breathe a sigh of relief.

The bouncer grabbed Jordan's arm and jerked him forward. Normally Jordan would have attempted to talk his way out of the confrontation. He wasn't, in the usual course of things, a combative man. But the bar had opened up to a free-for-all. Chairs flew around him, bottles and glasses were thrown. Men were shouting and punching and cursing.

Jordan locked his jaw. He needed to get the woman out of harm's way, and he needed to take his cohorts back to Buckhorn. Before he had time to really think about what he would do, he ducked under the bouncer's meaty arm and came up behind him. The guy was huge, easily four inches taller than Jordan's six foot one, with a neck the size of a tree trunk. Jordan gripped the man's fingers and applied just enough negative pressure for the big guy to issue a moan of pain. Jordan wrapped his free arm around the bouncer's throat and squeezed.

"Just hold still," Jordan said in disgust, wondering what the hell he should do now. He ducked a body that came staggering past, inadvertently hurting the bouncer further. Damn, things had gotten out of hand.

Jordan wasn't a fighter, but he had grown up with two older brothers and one younger. Being the pacifist in a family full of physical aggressors, he'd been taught to give as well as take. Not that he and his brothers had ever had any serious fistfights. But his brothers played as hard as they fought, so Jordan had learned how to hold his own.

Morgan, his second oldest brother, was built like a solid brick wall and Jordan had practiced up on him most of his life. There were few things that Morgan enjoyed more than a good skirmish. And though he was beyond fair, Morgan always finished as the victor.

Jordan knew how to handle the big ones. Morgan had generously seen to that.

Sirens sounded outside, adding to the confusion. In strangled tones, the bouncer demanded to be released, but Jordan ignored him, maintaining his awkward hold and refusing to lose the upper hand. Using the large man as a shield, Jordan turned to the woman and shouted, "Get away from here."

She hesitated for only a moment, sending a regretful look at the money scattered across the stage. Then her gray eyes met his and she nodded her agreement. But before she could go, her eyes widened and she looked beyond Jordan. He twisted just in time to avoid getting hit from behind. The bouncer ended up taking the brunt of the blow, which left him cursing and very disgruntled, but still very alert. Jordan raised his brows. It was a good thing he'd immobilized the big bruiser, because he wasn't at all certain he could have bested him face-to-face.

He turned back in time to see the woman scrambling up onto the stage. In her retreat, she gave Jordan a delectable view of her bottom in the skimpy costume. Despite his precarious position—having his arms filled with an outraged bouncer—Jordan felt his heartbeat accelerate at the luscious sight of her. She was almost to the curtain when several policemen charged through the doors.

With a feeling of dread, Jordan saw the officers draw their guns as they issued the clichéd order of *"everybody freeze."*

Zenny, Walt, Newton and the others were nowhere in sight, having evidently made a run for it when they heard the sirens. At least they'd managed to avoid this situation, Jordan thought. In fact, he'd be willing to bet they were already halfway back to Buckhorn, anxious to begin spreading tales of his night of debauchery. This was likely more excitement than any of the older citizens had experienced in many years, and the only thing that might compare would be the joy of telling others about it.

Jordan's thoughts were interrupted when a young officer climbed onto the stage and approached the dancer. She looked like she wanted to run, but instead she faced him with a defiant pose and began arguing. Dressed as she was, her attitude was more ludicrous than not. A mostly naked woman could hardly be taken seriously.

Jordan started toward her, bustling the bouncer along with him, meaning to intervene. But before he'd taken two steps another officer stepped in front of him. All around them, men were shouting curses and arguing, which did them no good at all. Having no choice, Jordan released the bouncer, who began shaking his hand and cursing and promising dire consequences. He was quickly handcuffed and urged into the crowd of men being corralled outside. The officer turned to Jordan with a frown.

Knowing there was no hope for it, Jordan merely held out his hands and suffered the unique experience of being handcuffed. Beside him, men attempted to argue their circumstances, and were shoved roughly out the door for their efforts. Jordan shook his head at the demeaning display while still keeping one eye on the woman. Someone, he thought, should at least offer to let her get dressed.

"You're not from around here, are you?" the officer asked Jordan.

"No, I'm from Buckhorn." He gave the admission grudgingly, but he already knew there was no way to keep this stupid contretemps from his brothers. They'd rib him about this for the rest of eternity.

The officer lifted a brow and grinned with a good deal of satisfaction. "That's a break. You can just wait in my car while I notify the sheriff of Buckhorn. He can deal with you himself and save me the trouble."

When the officer started to pull him away, Jordan asked, "The woman...?"

"I'd worry about my own hide if I was you," he said, then added, "That Buckhorn sheriff is one mean son of a bitch."

Since the sheriff was none other than his brother Morgan, Jordan was already well aware of that fact. He lost sight of the woman as he was escorted outside through the rain and into the back seat of a cruiser where he cursed his fate, his libido and his damned temper, which had chosen a hell of a bad time to display itself. The car he'd arrived in was long gone, proving his supposition that the others had headed home.

The car door opened again and an officer helped the woman inside. She faltered when she saw Jordan sitting there, staring at her in blank surprise. "Oh, Lord," she whispered with heartfelt distress. She dropped back into the seat and covered her face with her hands. "Just when I think the night can't get any worse...."

Jordan breathed in the scent of her rain-damp skin and hair, acutely aware of her frustration, her exhaustion. He settled into his seat and realized that despite how she felt, the night had just taken a dramatic turn for the better as far as he was concerned.

2

"YOU LIVE IN Buckhorn?" he asked, which was the only conclusion he could come up with for why she was now in the car with him.

When she didn't answer, the officer gave him a man-to-man look and said, "According to her license, she does."

Jordan leaned forward to see her face, but with her hands still covering it, that wasn't possible. He gently caught her wrists and tugged them down. Their handcuffs clinked together.

Softly, attempting to put her at ease, he asked, "Whereabouts? I've never seen you before." And he sure as certain would have remembered if he ever had. Even if she'd been fully clothed and doing something as mundane as shopping for groceries, he felt certain he'd have paid special attention to her. There was something about her that hit him on a gut level.

Just being this close to her now had his muscles cramping in a decidedly erotic way. Like the effects of prolonged foreplay, the sensation was pleasurable yet somewhat painful at the same time, because of the imposed restraint.

Their gazes met, his curious, hers wary and antagonistic. She looked away. "Where I live," she said under her breath, "is no concern of yours."

The officer answered again, disregarding her wishes for privacy. "You know that old farmhouse, out by the water tower? She moved in there."

The woman glared at the officer, who did manage to look a bit sheepish over his quick tongue. He leaned farther into the car to remove her handcuffs and place her purse in her lap. Jordan stared at her narrow wrists while she rubbed them, feeling his temper prick at the thought that she might have been hurt.

She wore no jewelry—no wedding band.

The officer spared him a glance. "If I remove your handcuffs, too, do you think you can behave yourself?"

It rankled, being treated like an unruly child, but Jordan was too busy staring at the woman to take too much offense. He silently held up his hands and waited to have them unlocked. The woman stared out her window past the officer, ignoring Jordan completely.

"What are we waiting for?" Jordan asked, before the officer could walk away.

"The chief agrees that Sheriff Hudson can deal with the both of you. Our jail is overcrowded as it is, and it's going to be a late night getting everyone's phone calls out of the way. Just sit tight. Hudson's already been called."

Jordan groaned softly. Morgan had his hands full taking care of Misty tonight. She was laid low with the nastiest case of flu Jordan had ever seen, and with their baby daughter to contend with, Morgan wouldn't appreciate being called out. Of course, his brother Gabe or one of his sisters-in-law, Honey or

Elizabeth, would gladly give a helping hand. But that meant they then ran the risk of getting the flu, too.

Jordan forced his gaze away from the woman and dropped his head back against the seat. "I'm never going to hear the end of this."

She shifted slightly away from him, though she was already pressed up against the door. Jordan swiveled his head just a bit to see her. The night was dark with no stars visible, no moonlight. Shadows played over her features and exaggerated her guarded frown. She looked quietly, disturbingly miserable. And she was shivering.

No wonder, he thought, calling himself three kinds of fool. The outfit she wore offered no protection at all from the rainy night air. Though it was September, a cool wet spell had rolled into Kentucky forcing everyone into slightly warmer clothes. Jordan studied her bare shoulders and slim naked limbs as he removed his jacket. It was damp around the collar, but still dry on the inside, and warm from his own body heat.

Aware of her efforts to ignore him, he held it out to her, his gaze intent. "Put this on," he told her, using his most cajoling tone. "You're shivering."

Very slowly, she turned her head and looked at him with the most distant, skeptical expression he'd ever seen on a female face. "Why are you talking like that?"

Jordan started in surprise. "Like what?" he asked, not quite so softly or cajoling.

Her frown was filled with distrust...and accusation. "Like you're trying to seduce me. Like a man talks to a woman when they're alone together in bed."

Jordan couldn't have been more floored by her direct attack if she'd clobbered him. Totally bemused, he opened his mouth, but nothing came out.

She made a sound of disgust. "You can stop wasting your time. I'm not interested. And no, I don't want your jacket."

Taken off guard, Jordan frowned. All his life, women had told him he had the most compelling voice. He could lull a wounded bear to sleep or talk grown men out of a fistfight. At the ripe old age of thirty-three, he'd garnered a half dozen wedding proposals from women who said they loved to just listen to him talk, especially in bed.

But right then, at this particular moment, he didn't even think about trying to be persuasive. He even forgot that he *could* be persuasive.

"Don't be a fool," he growled. "You'll end up catching your death running around near naked like that."

Her arms crossed over her middle and her neck stiffened at his exasperated tone. A heavy beat of silence passed before she rounded on him. Her eyes weren't cool now. They were bright and hot with anger.

"I can't believe you got me into this fix," she nearly shouted, "then have the nerve to try to seduce me and—"

"I wasn't trying to seduce you, damn it!"

"—and to criticize me!"

Distracted by the way her crossed arms hefted her breasts a little higher, Jordan was slow to respond. He managed to drag his gaze up to her very angry face again, and he scowled. "*I* got you into this fix? Honey, I'm the one who was trying to help you out!"

She thrust her jaw toward him in clear challenge.

She was so close, her sweet hot breath pelted his face. "I'm not your damn *honey*, mister, and I didn't need your help. I deal with Larry in one way or another nearly every night. He's a regular at the bar—a regular drunk and a regular pain in the butt. But I know how to handle him." Her lip curled, and she added with contempt, "Obviously, you don't."

Jordan let his hand holding the jacket drop to the seat between them. Never in his life had he been at such a loss for words. He rubbed his chin, scrutinizing her until she squirmed. Good. Her discomfort, in the face of her hostility, gave him a heady dose of satisfaction.

"Ah." He cocked one brow. "I think I understand now."

"I seriously doubt that."

He shrugged. "I suppose any woman with enough guts to display herself as you did tonight must know how to handle the pathetic drunks who want to grope her. I'm sorry I interfered. Would Larry have given you a bigger tip?"

She choked on an outraged breath. "You hypocrite! I had you pegged from the start. You sit there and condemn me, yet you were at the bar, weren't you? You'll gladly watch, even as you look down your nose at the entertainment."

Jordan leaned closer, too, drawn to her like a magnet, wishing he could lift her into his lap and hold her close and feel all that angry passion flush against his body. She practically vibrated with her fury, and for some fool reason it turned him on like the most potent aphrodisiac.

"I was there," Jordan said, "to protest the place, not to support your little display."

Her eyes widened and her chest heaved; Jordan couldn't help it, he stared at her breasts. They were more than a handful, shimmering with her frustration, creamy pale and looking so soft. His palms itched with the need to scoop those luscious breasts out of her bodice and weigh them in his hands, to flick her nipples with his thumbs until they stiffened, until she moaned.

He swallowed hard and met her gaze, knowing his look was covetous, knowing that she knew it, too.

"So," she said, and to his interest, she sounded a bit breathless despite her efforts at acerbity, "you're a vigilante? One of those crazy people who protests all the sinners, people who drink or dance or have fun of any kind?"

"Not at all." They were both so close now, a mere inch separated them. She wasn't backing off any more than he was, and her bravado served as another source of excitement. He'd never met a woman like her.

Jordan felt the clash of wills and the draw of sensual interest. "My only concern," he murmured, distracted by her warmth, her scent, "is the inebriated men who leave the bar and enter my county. *Your* county. They've caused a few problems which I'd like to see taken care of before someone ends up hurt or even killed."

Her gaze dropped to his mouth. Jordan drew a deep breath, trying to remember what it was he had to say. "I had intended to talk to the owner, nothing more.

But then, I didn't realize you liked being felt up by Larry."

Her gaze jerked back to his. Her bottom lip quivered before she stilled it, making Jordan wonder if it was caused by upset at his nasty words—*why* was he being nasty, damn it?—or from the distinct chill of the night. He felt the first nigglings of shame for baiting her. In the normal course of things, he never intentionally insulted women. He was gentle and understanding. But this wasn't a normal night, she wasn't the average woman, and his reactions to her were as far from the expected as he could get.

"He touched my leg," she said succinctly, "and before he would have touched anything else, Gus would have stopped him."

"Gus?" A tiny flare of jealousy took him by surprise.

"The bouncer. The one you..."

"Ah." Jordan saw a hint of color sweep over her face and touched her cheek with his fingertips, gently smoothing a damp curl aside. "The big bruiser I stopped from knocking me out. Why the hell was he attacking me, anyway?"

She didn't protest his touch. They were both breathing too hard, too fast. She lifted one delicate shoulder in a way that made her breasts shift, teasing him with the possibility of gaining a peek at her taut nipples. He was disappointed to see she stayed securely inside the bodice. Jordan shook his head and tried to force himself to concentrate on their conversation, impossible as that seemed.

"He doesn't know you," she said. "And you

looked—'' She peeked up at him, a slight frown marring her brown. "Well, you looked furious."

"I was furious." His voice dropped to a whisper, making her eyes, shadowed and cautious, widen on his face. "I thought someone was going to hurt you."

Her lips parted.

Outside the car, one man struggling against being arrested fetched up against the door closest to the woman. She jumped, letting out a startled gasp. Without even thinking about it, Jordan clasped her shoulder, offering comfort and reassurance. Her soft skin tempted him and it was all he could do to keep the touch impersonal, to keep from caressing her. But she also felt cool against the warmth of his hand, making him frown.

A lot of activity was going on around them, though he hadn't been aware of it moments before. Above the din of complaints and drunken shouts, Jordan heard the sheriff arguing that he'd been called one time too many to the bar, and now he was forced to actually do something, just so he could get some peace.

Apparently that *something* was a series of arrests, and it didn't matter that Jordan hadn't been drinking, that he hadn't started the fight, and that he'd had nothing to do with the other numerous times the disgruntled sheriff had been summoned.

"Nice place you work at." Jordan continued to smooth his fingers over her skin, unable to force himself to move away from her.

"It pays the bills," was her straightforward reply, then she suddenly seemed to realize his touch and turned to glare at him.

Jordan again held up the coat. "Do you really want my brother to see you looking like that?"

"Your brother?"

"The Buckhorn sheriff. If I know Morgan, he's liable to be here any minute. I'm sure I'll get the brunt of his anger, but believe me, there'll be a heady dose for you, too, since he'd had his evening all planned and it didn't include a jaunt out into the rainy night. Wouldn't you rather be wearing a little more armor than lace and fringe?"

Her hands knotted together in her lap. "Do you think he'll keep us for the night?"

She looked so fragile and delicate, so damn young, Jordan had a hard time reconciling the confident, aloof vamp she'd been on the stage with the concerned, shivering woman she was now. She simply didn't strike him as a person hardened to life, a woman brazen enough to be comfortable with her earlier display.

It was Jordan's turn to shrug. "Who knows? He has no tolerance for ignorance, regardless of the fact we're related. But then again, he's very fair and you and I weren't to blame for what happened in there."

Her glare said differently. Jordan smiled. "Okay, so you think I was to blame. Is that any reason to sit there freezing?" He traced the line of her throat with one fingertip. "Your skin is like ice."

A slight shudder ran through her and her eyes closed. Jordan stared, feeling what she felt, the connection, the instantaneous sexual charge. Like a touch of lightning, it sizzled along his every nerve ending, making him so acutely aware of her he hurt. He'd never known anything like it and he had no idea how to deal with it. He wanted, quite frankly, to pull her down into the seat and strip off her costume and cover her with his body. He wanted to warm her with his heat. He wanted to take her, right now, right here, to brand her with his touch.

There were no gentle words of admiration in his mind, no thoughts of cautious seduction. He felt savage, and it shook him.

After a shuddering breath, she moved away from his caressing fingers and accepted his coat. He helped her to slip it on, watching her contortions in the limited space of the back seat, seeing the thrust of her breasts as she slipped first one arm though, then the other. She lifted slightly to settle it behind her, and Jordan petted the material down her narrow back, all the way to the base of her spine. She felt supple and firm and he relished the sound of her quickened breath.

He smiled at how the sleeves completely hid her hands, curiously satisfied at seeing her in his coat and feeling somewhat barbaric because of it. She trembled so badly she couldn't quite manage the buttons. Jordan brushed her small, chilled hands away and did them up for her. In a voice affected by being so close to her, he whispered, "Better?"

"Yes, thank you."

Her voice, too, sounded huskier than usual, proving to Jordan that he wasn't sinking alone. No. Whatever strange affliction he felt, she felt it, too.

The urge to touch her again was strong, and he gave into it, tucking a damp curl behind her ear. Her hair was as soft as her skin, baby fine, intriguing. It was cut into various-length curls that moved and bounced when she turned her head. Along her nape, the hair had pulled into adorable little ringlets. He lifted those small curls out of the collar of his coat. "I'm Jordan Sommerville," he said, and heard the increasing rush of her breath.

Staring down at her hands, she replied, "Georgia Barnes."

"Georgia? As in a Georgia peach?"

"Don't start." Then she blinked and looked up at him. "Sommerville? I thought you said Sheriff Hudson was your brother?"

"Half brother," Jordan explained. He felt the old bitterness rise up, nearly choking him.

Her head tilted in a curious way. "The sheriff is your younger brother?"

"No. Morgan is the second oldest, right behind Sawyer." Jordan didn't feel like explaining. If he was in Buckhorn, he wouldn't have to, because everyone there knew everyone else's business. In fact, he decided she must either be very new to the area or very isolated, not to have already heard the stories herself.

There was no disapproval in her tone when she asked, "Your mother has been married twice?"

Jordan sighed, seeing no hope for it. At least Georgia—what a name, probably just used as a stage name—was talking to him. "My mother's first husband died in the service after giving her two sons, Sawyer and Morgan. She married my father, but not for long because he became a miserable drunk shortly after the wedding."

He saw her eyes glittering in surprise, saw her soft mouth open. Jordan cupped her chin and touched her bottom lip with his thumb, hungry for the taste of her, as unlikely as that seemed. He barely knew her, and for the most part he didn't like what he did know, but he felt as though he'd wanted her forever.

Without meaning to, without even wanting to reveal so much, he added, "By all accounts, my father was the type of man who would have loved this bar—as well as that little show of yours." Slowly, he looked her over in his too large coat, her honey-brown hair wispy and curled with perspiration and rain, her flamboyant makeup smudged.

Her slender bare thigh rested only a few inches beside his, taunting him with its nearness. His hand was large enough that he could cover the entire front of her thigh with his splayed fingers. He could caress her skin, parting her legs as he inched higher and higher until he cupped her, felt her heat, her softness. The material of her bodysuit would offer no obstruction at all. He could...

He muttered a low curse. With the drizzling rain outside sealing them in, her musky scent seemed to permeate his brain. It filled him with lust so strong he felt it in his heartbeat, tasted it on his tongue. He'd never been thrown so off balance in his entire life.

"My father," Jordan said in a raw voice, "would have been right up there with the others, sweetheart, throwing money on the stage, urging you on, and doing his damndest to buy your favors. But seeing you tonight..." He hesitated and his hand opened on the back of her head as he thrust his fingers through her silky hair, urging her closer, watching her pupils expand wildly. "...I can almost forgive him for that."

Jordan's words trailed off into a whisper as her eyes slowly closed, her lips parting on a hungry breath. Her invitation was clear, and he leaned toward her, already growing hard in anticipation of taking her mouth. He couldn't believe this was happening, and he couldn't stop it.

She gave a soft moan as he kissed the very corner of her lips, and another when he tilted his head and brushed his mouth over hers. Her lips parted on the third moan and Jordan took her, his tongue immediately sinking deep, his mind shutting down on everything except the hot taste of her, the wild, savage way she made him feel.

A loud rapping on the window jarred him out of his lust-fogged stupor.

Georgia jumped back, gasping, one hand at her throat as her face drained of color. It didn't take a rocket scientist to know she was mortified, that she'd been as carried away as Jordan. He leaned past her to see his largest brother scowling through the window.

Morgan's hair was plastered to his skull, his face was unshaven and he wore a plain T-shirt and jeans, testimony to the fact that he'd been at home, not on call. He must have driven at top speed, Jordan realized, to have gotten to the bar so quickly.

Morgan's requisite badass look was firmly in place, the one that had kept Buckhorn citizens in line for some time now—the same look that made them all respect him as a man fully capable of handling any situation.

Not in the least daunted by that black expression, Jordan shoved his door open and stepped out of the car, addressing Morgan over the roof. "You've got about the lousiest damn timing of any man I've ever known!"

Morgan, red-eyed and looking mean, made a sound

reminiscent of a snarl. "I'm leaving that distinction to you, Jordan. And you better have one helluva good excuse for this, otherwise I'm liable to kick your ass all the way home—where my sick wife and fussing baby girl are waiting."

Jordan prepared to blast him with his own ire, made hotter out of unreasoning sexual frustration. But he'd barely gotten two sputtering words out before Georgia shoved her door open, making Morgan back up a pace. She climbed out of the police car, faced him with a serene expression fit for a queen, and said, "You can handle this little family squabble later. I, for one, would like to get this over with so I can get home."

IT WAS ALL Georgia could do to keep herself from trembling. The man staring down at her had the most ferocious demeanor she'd ever witnessed on man or rabid dog. Besides being enormous, he was dark and so layered in thick muscle she felt dwarfed beside him.

And here she'd thought Jordan was huge.

Actually, the two men were of a similar height, but where Jordan appeared athletic, lean and toned, this man looked like he could eat gravel for breakfast.

Despite her resolve, she began quaking like a wet Chihuahua. And then suddenly Jordan was at her side.

"Knock it off, Morgan. You're scaring her."

When Jordan's hands settled on her shoulders, she didn't move away. She should have, being that Jordan had the power to turn her knees to jelly and her insides to fire. *She'd let him kiss her.* The reality of that wasn't to be borne.

The man had the most sinfully seductive voice she'd ever heard, even when insulting and baiting her. She'd done the unthinkable, all because his voice had softened her, melting away her will and her resolve. She scowled at herself, feeling the shame claw at her. She didn't like men—not at all. Not for friends, certainly not for lovers.

Most definitely not for a one-night stand, which from what she could deduce, was what Jordan Sommerville was after. He'd made no pretense of liking her or approving of her in any way. The arrogant jerk.

She forced herself to meet the sheriff's gaze. "Actually, you're not. Scaring me, that is." The lie sounded credible even to her own ears, though neither man seemed to believe her. "So if it's all the same to you I'd just as soon get out of this rain and get going."

Morgan snorted, eyeing her with a mix of clear annoyance, and perhaps a touch of approval. "So anxious to spend a night in jail, are you?"

She nearly staggered. "Jail? But..." Her stomach suddenly felt queasy, her knees weak. She couldn't, absolutely couldn't stay away all night. Swallowing hard, and hating what she had to say even before the words left her mouth, she forced herself to meet the sheriff's gaze. "I have to go home. Tonight."

Morgan's eyes narrowed. "Got a husband waiting for you?"

She shook her head and felt a raindrop slither down her nose. "Two children."

Jordan's hands bit reflexively into her shoulders. "*What?*"

Georgia felt hemmed in by testosterone. The sheriff looked too grim by half, and she could feel the tension radiating off Jordan. She shifted her shoulders slightly at the pressure of his fingers and he loosened his hold, then turned her around to face him.

"You have kids?" His eyes were like green fire.

She lifted her chin. "Yes."

The shock on his face was replaced with disgust. "Where the hell is your husband?"

She owed him nothing, certainly no explanations. "Ex-husband. And I have no idea." Jordan's brows smoothed out, and she added, "But wherever he is, I hope he stays there. Now, are you done with your interrogation?"

The sheriff snorted. "Maybe you should ask me that."

Jordan, no longer looking like a thundercloud, pulled her behind his back. Georgia couldn't see around him, but she heard him plain enough as he addressed his brother.

"You're not going to arrest her, Morgan, and you know it, so quit taking your bad temper out on her."

The sheriff seemed to be spoiling for a fight. "Or what?"

"Or I'll tell Misty."

Georgia had no idea who Misty was or why her name would make the sheriff relent, but that's exactly what happened. Sheriff Hudson still sounded annoyed, but no longer so angry. "It's a lousy night for you to do this to me, Jordan."

"Yeah, well, it wasn't my idea for you to be called, you know."

"No? What was your idea? To start an all out brawl? I thought you came along to see that there was no trouble, not to insure that there was."

"I didn't cause the trouble. I was only..."

His words trailed off as Georgia stepped around him and headed for the bar. If the fool men wanted to stand around in the rain and discuss the situation to death, that was fine with her. But now that she felt certain she wouldn't be locked up, she had a better way to spend her time.

Before she'd gone five feet, Jordan's hand closed around her elbow. "Where do you think you're going?"

With a sigh, she drew up short and turned to face him. She shook back one of the long sleeves of his jacket to free a hand, and then shoved her hair out of her face. Her makeup, she knew, was a disaster.

Not that she cared.

Jordan's hold on her arm was gentle. His light brown hair hung over his brow, now more wet than otherwise, and his eyes reflected the bar lights, appearing almost...hungry. She looked quickly away. "I've got money on the stage. If I don't get it now, Bill will abscond with it and I'll have wasted the night for nothing. Since you two don't seem in a big hurry to rush off, and the other sheriff is apparently done inside—"

"Bill?"

He did seem to get hung up on every male name she mentioned. "The owner of the bar. The man you came to see before you got...sidetracked." She tried to pull away but Jordan wasn't letting go.

He turned to Morgan. "Can you give us just a moment?"

"Just." Morgan didn't look happy over the concession, but then, she doubted that this one ever looked happy. "Malone will only stay in bed when I'm there to force her to it. Otherwise, you know how she is. She'll be up and running around, making herself feverish again...."

"We'll be quick. Why don't you go warm up the car?"

With a shrug, the sheriff turned away. Georgia watched him go with relief. "Who's Malone?"

"His wife, Misty."

So it was his wife that Jordan had threatened him with? That seemed curious to Georgia.

"Why does he call her Malone...never mind." Disgusted with herself, Georgia turned away. She didn't care about these men or their strange ways. She walked briskly into the bar, doing her best to ignore the warm touch of Jordan's hand on her arm as he kept pace with her. Even through his coat sleeve, she could feel his strength, his heat. And for some absurd reason, she reacted to it. He had her thinking things she hadn't thought in years, contemplating pleasures she was certain didn't even exist.

Bill was just scooping up the money off the stage when they walked in. Jordan released her and she marched forward, saying sweetly, "Why thank you, Bill. I so appreciate you looking after my money for me."

Bill had the kind of slick good looks that he assumed would get him anything he wanted from women. To Georgia, his perfectly styled blond hair, dark blue eyes, and capped teeth only emphasized what a fraud he was. She didn't trust him one iota and never would.

Bill flashed her a surprised look. "Georgia! I thought you were gone."

"Almost." She stuck out her hand expectantly and Bill tucked the money closer to his chest. "I'm waiting," she said, well used to having to deal with Bill and his miserly ways. Like most men, he had a self-serving streak a mile wide, a selfish attitude whenever it came to money and he didn't hesitate to screw someone when he thought he could get away with it.

"What about the damages to my bar?" he blustered, and cast a nasty look at Jordan Sommerville.

Georgia glanced at Jordan, too, and saw that he had an expression almost as fierce as his brother's. It was the same look he'd worn earlier, when Larry had held on to her wrist. He'd said he was furious...because he thought she might be hurt.

She turned away. "That wasn't my doing, Bill, and you know it. Take up your grievances with the boys locked away. But give me my money." When Bill still dithered, looking undecided as to whether or not he had to obey, she narrowed her eyes and said, "You know I can dance anywhere, Bill. Don't push me. I need the money."

With a foul curse that would have embarrassed her as little as a month ago, Bill thrust the wad of bills into her hands. Most of them were ones, but altogether, it should amount up to a hundred dollars or more, money she needed to make repairs to the house she'd recently bought. With a sugary sweet, utterly false smile, she muttered, "Thank you."

She turned to Jordan, saw his look of contempt, and sniffed. Sanctimonious jerk. "I'm ready if you are."

Jordan held the saloon door open for her and kept

stride with her on the way to the large black sport utility vehicle his brother drove. Some official car, she thought, eyeing the shiny black four-wheel-drive Bronco.

The two sheriffs had been talking, but as she and Jordan neared the vehicle, they parted ways. Sheriff Hudson got behind the wheel.

The rain had almost let up, but a chill had settled in that seemed to seep into her bones. Her bare legs were freezing and she'd somehow managed to step into a puddle, getting both feet soaked. She would have changed clothes, but the sheriff was in an obvious hurry to get going and she didn't want to push her luck. The quicker she got this over with, the quicker she could get home. She was so weary she ached all the way down to her toes and more than anything she needed a good night's sleep.

But once she got home, there would be chores to do. If she didn't get some of the laundry taken care of, they'd all be running around naked. She had no doubt the sink was full of dishes, and there were bills that had to be paid before she lost her utilities.

She was so drawn into her thoughts, she nearly tripped over Jordan when he held the front door of the Bronco open for her. Belatedly, she realized he expected her to ride to the sheriff's station sandwiched between two overwhelmingly male bodies.

"I'll sit in back," she offered, hoping she sounded merely casual, not concerned.

Jordan narrowed his gaze on her. "You'll ride up front. I want to talk to you."

He appeared determined and unrelenting, so she looked past him to see the sheriff. "Excuse me," she said, and Morgan Hudson turned his head to look at her, then lifted one black brow. "I'd prefer to ride in the back like any other criminal being arrested."

Morgan opened his mouth to say something, but snapped it shut when she yelped. Jordan's hands were secure on her waist as he literally tossed her into the front seat and climbed in beside her too quickly for her to do anything about it. He looked at his brother and said, "Drive," and with a slight, barely suppressed chuckle, the good sheriff did just that.

3

GEORGIA STEAMED, she was so angry. At herself as much as at the two outrageous, oversized men. They'd driven a few minutes in silence when she finally couldn't hold it in any longer and growled, "I don't like you."

Jordan started, evidently surprised that she'd spoken after being quiet for so long. And Morgan grinned. She'd already decided that the sheriff was either frowning or grinning—there wasn't much middle ground.

"Which of us are you talking to?" Morgan asked.

She was just disgruntled enough to bark, "Both." Unfortunately, Jordan seemed unfazed by her pique and Morgan was amused.

She was still pondering what to do and how to get everything done tonight when Jordan gave Morgan directions to her home, telling her without words that he was indeed familiar with the old farmhouse she'd bought.

But more important than that, she realized they were taking her straight home, rather than to the station.

"Excuse me," she said, giving her attention to the sheriff while doing her best to ignore Jordan pressed up against her side, "but if you're only going to take me home, why did I just leave my car at the bar? Do you realize what a nuisance this will be now for me to get it?"

Morgan shrugged. "Don't worry about your car. We'll take care of it in the morning. Isn't that right, Jordan?"

Jordan made a noncommittal sound that she wasn't interested in deciphering. "I don't *want* you to take care of it!"

Jordan stared out his window. Morgan glanced at her, then back to the road. "Not much choice, now. There was a lot going on. I figured it'd be easier this way, rather than hassling with the arresting sheriff. He wanted you two taken off, so I took you off. And as to that, I suppose I should give you a ticket or something." She watched the sheriff rub his thick neck, as if pondering a difficult predicament. "You see, the thing is, Jordan said you weren't to blame and I've never known him to tell me a pickle. But I gotta say, I am curious as hell as to why you were picked up, why you were there in the first place, and why you're dressed that way."

He leaned around to see Jordan, and added, "And what the hell you've got to do with it."

Though she knew the sheriff was only trying to distract her, Georgia stiffened. "He has nothing to do with me! But he did attempt to intervene…well, sort of…"

Jordan made another exasperated sound and interrupted. "I don't need you to explain for me, Georgia."

She shrugged, stung by his biting tone. "Fine." Crossing her arms, she leaned back in the seat, silent again.

Morgan began to whistle. After a moment, he said thoughtfully, "I think I have it figured out."

"Morgan," Jordan said by way of warning.

"You're a dancer at the bar, right?" At her stiff nod, he continued. "And Jordan here got a little too enthused over your...skill. Understandable. Although Jordan is a little slow on the uptake sometimes, at least where women are concerned—"

"Oh, for God's sake."

Georgia listened, fascinated despite herself.

"You see," Morgan said in something of a whisper, leaning toward Georgia, "in the last few years my brothers and I have all tied the knot. All except Jordan, and that leaves him sort of vulnerable to all the hungry single ladies looking to get hitched. He's so busy trying to fend them off, he's forgotten just how pleasant a nice, warm woman can be."

Georgia blinked. "I really don't think—"

"It's obvious to me that old Jordan here has lost his finesse. I'd be willing to bet he tried to defend your honor or something like that, is that right?"

Jordan growled, but Georgia paid him and his nasty temper no mind. This night had been endless and she'd had just about enough. "You think, perhaps, that I don't have any honor to defend just because I work for a living?"

Morgan surprised her by shaking his head. "Not at all. I don't make those type of assumptions about ladies. Malone'd have my head if I did, seeing as I once made a horrid assumption about her."

Before she could ponder that particular scenario too long, Jordan slapped one hand down on the dash and twisted in his seat to face them both. "You want the nitty-gritty details, Morgan? Is that it?"

"Of course."

Jordan glared at his brother, and Georgia could feel his hot breath as he leaned around her. Being stuck between these two big oafs was not her idea of fun. She pressed farther back in her seat.

"All right, fine." The words were ground out from between clenched teeth. "She finished dancing and some bozo started groping her leg. He wouldn't quit when she asked him to and I stepped in. Unnecessarily, it would seem, at least according to Ms. Barnes."

Slowly, Georgia turned toward him. She heard his brother mutter, *"uh-oh"* under his breath, yet all her attention was now on Jordan.

"For your information," she said in a slow, precise tone, "I work all week in the bar as a waitress. I deal with those bozos day in and day out. I know them, and I know just how to get them to back off. *Without* throwing any punches or starting any riots."

"Uh..." Morgan said, attempting to intervene, "Jordan actually punched someone?"

"Several someones!"

"Only two."

Morgan cleared his throat. "You dress like that to serve drinks? You must make some hellacious tips."

Contrary to what she'd just said, Georgia felt like throwing her own punch. "I dress like this to dance on the weekends because it pays a lot better than serving drinks through the week, and unlike some people—" she fried Jordan a look "—I have obligations, and have to do whatever I can to make ends meet."

The car slowed as Morgan pulled into her driveway. Even as angry as she was, a curious peace settled over her at being home. She'd loved the big old house on sight and dreamed of renovating it into a home her kids could finally be proud of, a home that would last them forever.

It needed work, no denying that. But the yard was spacious, giving the kids plenty of room to play. And the air out here in the country was clean, fresh, putting new color in her mother's cheeks. The house represented everything Georgia had ever wanted or needed for her family.

Her fist curled around the strap of her purse, now filled with the money that had been thrown onstage. With a little luck, a lot of determination, and enough fortitude, she *could* make everything right. She had to. Her options were sorely limited.

Morgan turned the car off and Georgia, pulled from her thoughts, realized Jordan was staring at her mouth. Again. Heat rushed through her like a tidal wave, stealing her breath until she nearly choked.

How did he keep doing this to her? He'd made it clear he didn't approve of her, yet he wanted her. And if she was honest with herself, she was far too aware of him as a man. *Absurd.* She'd sworn off men!

"It looks to me," Morgan said softly, "as if a couple of small obligations have been waiting for you."

"What?" Georgia twisted around at the considering tone of the sheriff's voice, only to see her son and daughter standing anxiously in the open doorway of the house, their noses practically pressed to the storm door. She knew in an instant that something was very wrong. They should have been long in bed. Her mother never let them to the door without her.

In a single heartbeat her distraction with Jordan disappeared, as did her exhaustion. All that remained was mind-numbing fear.

"Oh, God." Georgia practically climbed over Jordan, who did his best to get the door open for her and to get out of her way. He didn't even complain when her elbow clipped him in the nose and she stepped on his foot.

"Georgia, wait!"

She heard his alarmed tone as he followed her from the car, heard Morgan talking low, his words concerned. And then her daughter Lisa, only six years old, threw the front door open and dashed across the yard in her long nightgown. Georgia forgot all about the men.

"MOMMY!"

Jordan nearly slipped on the wet grass. Knowing she was a mother and seeing a little girl address her as such were two entirely different things. His heart punched hard against his ribs when Georgia dropped to her knees, unconcerned with the soggy ground, and caught her daughter up to her.

"Lisa, what is it, honey? What's wrong?"

The little girl was crying too hard to make sense. A queer feeling of resentment—she'd left the child to dance in a bar, for God's sake—and tenderness, seeing her now, holding the child so closely, made Jordan almost breathless. He stepped closer and with a hiccup, the little girl looked up at him. She had huge brown eyes with spiked wet lashes and was about the cutest thing he'd ever seen.

Keeping a wary gaze on him, the little girl mumbled, "Grandma is sick. She won't wake up."

"Oh, my God!"

Just that quick, Georgia was back on her feet. She'd picked up the little girl and was running hell-bent across the lawn. Her high heels sank into the ground, hindering her a bit, but in no way holding her back.

Jordan rushed after her, aware of Morgan right behind him. He followed her down a short hall as she called out, "Mom!" in a heart-wrenching panicked voice.

Lisa clung to Georgia's shoulders and said in a wavering voice, "She's in her room."

They passed a family room with a television playing and every light on, toys all over the floor, then a dining room that held only one rickety table—still covered with dishes.

At the end of the hall, to the right, was a kitchen, and to the left, Georgia threw open a door then halted. Jordan could see her heaving, see the rigidity of her shoulders. Slowly, she set the girl on her feet and moved forward. "Mom?"

Jordan watched the little girl move to a corner, trying to make herself invisible. Beyond Georgia, lying in a rumpled bed, a slender woman of about sixty rested on her back, her eyes closed, her chest barely moving—until she started coughing.

Lisa cried. Jordan didn't know what the hell to do. Then Morgan was there and he went down on one knee in front of Lisa. "Hi, there. I'm the sheriff and a friend of your mom's. Are you okay?"

Lisa covered her face with her hands, hiding, and then she nodded. Seeing that Morgan had things under control there, at least as much as was possible, Jordan stepped close to Georgia and knelt by the bed. She was busy checking her mother over, her movements efficient and quick.

She glanced at Jordan. "We have to get her to the hospital. She has weak lungs and it looks like she's gotten a bad cold or something."

Jordan frowned in concern. "A cold can do this to her?"

"Yes." Georgia's voice was clipped as she moved to a portable oxygen tank and dragged it to her mother's bedside. As she sat beside her mother and pulled her into a sitting position, the older woman's eyes opened. Again, she started coughing.

"It's all right now, Mom. I'm going to take you to the hospital.

"I'm sorry, honey—"

"Hey, none of that! I love you, remember?" She glanced at Jordan. "You're going to have to take us since you left my car behind." Then, as if just realizing it, her eyes widened in alarm and she said, "Lisa, where's Adam?"

A small towheaded child peeked around the doorframe.

"They're not used to men in the house," Georgia explained, then gave her son a small smile. "Come here, sweetie. It's okay. Grandma's going to be fine."

With the oxygen over her face, the older woman did seem to be breathing easier. She kept dozing off, which alarmed Jordan, but Georgia was holding it all together. The little boy inched his way in the door. He looked to be around four and clung to his mother's knee, hiding his face in her lap.

Jordan felt thunderstruck, and at that moment, he almost hated himself.

With renewed purpose, he stood. "I can carry her out to the Bronco. Morgan—"

"I'll call it in," Morgan said before Jordan could finish. He smiled at the little girl and smoothed a large hand over her head. "Can you find some shoes and a jacket for you and your brother?"

She peeked between her fingers, then nodded.

"Good girl."

Georgia smiled an absent thanks at Morgan. "Hang on, Mom. We'll have you there in no time."

Jordan knelt beside her and added his own arm to support her mother. "Why don't you get her coat and shoes for her? I'll do this."

Georgia hesitated, her eyes on her mother's face. "Her lungs are weak from emphysema. Sometimes, if she overdoes it, she needs the oxygen so we always keep it handy. She knows—" Her voice broke and frustrated tears filled her eyes. Angrily, she swiped them away. "She knows that any kind of illness for her is serious. But...she never complains."

Jordan watched her struggle to pull herself together. He covered her hand on the oxygen mask and asked, "Are you all right?"

Lips tightly pressed together, she nodded, then pushed to her feet. She found her mother's slippers beneath the bed. When she started looking around the room, Jordan changed his mind on the coat.

"Let's just wrap her in a blanket. It'll be easier for her, and the hospital will put her in a gown when she gets there anyway." Jordan didn't say it out loud, but judging by the difficulty her mother had breathing, he thought she might have pneumonia. With his own brother being a doctor, he'd seen enough cases of it. Plus her skin was pale and dry and too warm, indicating a high fever.

Georgia took a deep breath and wrapped her mother in a pretty quilt. Jordan saw the tears glisten in her eyes again and knew he'd made a horrible mistake.

IT HADN'T taken long for them to be on their way. With the combined efforts of Morgan and Jordan, things had just fallen into place. They were obviously men accustomed to taking charge. Georgia didn't know how she felt about that, but she did know she was glad not to be alone.

Lisa and Adam were buckled into the front seat with Morgan, thoroughly distracted from any worries as Morgan let them play with his radio and turn on his lights. It amazed her that a man so large, so commanding, could summon up such a gentle tone for children. Right now, as he smiled at Adam, he looked like a big pushover, when her first impression of him would never have allowed for such a possibility.

He'd already spoken with the hospital and they were ready and waiting for them to arrive. The flashing lights, which amused her kids, were necessary; Morgan drove well past the speed limit. But at this time of night, the streets were almost clear of traffic.

"It's usually about an hour's drive to the hospital." Jordan watched her closely as he spoke, but then, he'd hardly taken his gaze off her since she'd first noticed him at the bar. "At least from our house. But I'd say you're fifteen minutes closer, and with Morgan driving and no cars on the road, it shouldn't take much longer."

Georgia realized he was trying to put her at ease. She appreciated his efforts. Morgan's, too. The kids, after their initial bout of shyness and upset, had taken to him with hardly any reserve. He had an easy way about him that would naturally draw kids.

She had a feeling Jordan would be the same when he wasn't busy tending to her mother's care. She'd seen how he'd looked at her children, the softness in his eyes. He was a man of contradictions—harsh one minute, soft the next. Always strong and confident.

At the moment, with her knees shaking and her heart beating too fast, she resented his strength even as she relied on it. *She* had to be strong. And she never wanted to depend on another man for anything.

They sat in the back, her mother propped between them on the carpeted floor of the storage area. Georgia supported her mother with an arm around her waist, offering her shoulder to lean on.

Streetlamps glowed, their lights flashing into the moving car with a strobe effect. They cast dark, shifting shadows over Jordan's profile, but in no way detracted from his look of genuine concern. He was an incredibly handsome man, Georgia decided, and obviously very caring.

"Almost there," he said with a reassuring smile. "Just hang on." His mesmerizing voice soothed her as nothing else could. Even her mother, dozing and waking every few minutes, wasn't immune to it. Georgia held her close, but it was Jordan's hand she gripped like a lifeline, his voice that occasionally coerced her eyes open.

Georgia leaned close and kissed her mother's cheek. Everything would be all right. She had to believe that.

JORDAN KEPT HOLD of the woman's limp hand while watching her closely for any signs of distress. Her breathing was still ragged, occasionally racked by harsh coughing, but the oxygen had helped. That, and the fact that she knew she was almost at the hospital.

Georgia looked like hell. Though she tried to hide it, her own distress far outweighed her mother's. At that moment, Jordan wanted so badly to hold her close, to protect her. There seemed to be so much he hadn't understood. Her house was a shambles, inside and out. It had potential, but it would take a lot of sweat and money to make it what it could be.

Her children, adorable little moppets who had taken a cautious liking to Morgan, had her look about them. Lisa had the same golden-brown hair, though long enough to be in a braid, and Adam's hair was pale blond. They both had brown eyes, not Georgia's gray-blue, but the intensity in their gazes was the same as hers.

How the hell did she keep it all together? Between being a single parent of two young children, and her mother's health, not to mention the work needed on her house, she had her hands full.

He couldn't keep his gaze off her and glanced at her again just as she rubbed one tear-filled eye with a fist. She'd done that several times, refusing to let the tears fall, never mind that she had good reason, that most women would have bowed under the stress of the night. Her makeup was an absolute mess, leaving dark smudges on her cheeks and all around her eyes. Jordan reached into his pocket and retrieved a hanky.

"Hey," he said softly, and Georgia pulled her gaze away from her mother long enough to send him a questioning look.

He reached over and used the edge of the cotton hanky to wipe her eyes. "You look like a Halloween cat," he teased, and she gave him the first sincere smile he'd seen. It about stopped his heart. In that moment, with smeared makeup, rain-frazzled hair and a red nose, she was the most beautiful woman he'd ever seen.

Taking the hanky from him, she scrubbed at her face, removing the worst of the smudges. "I hate this stupid makeup, but Bill insists." She grinned at her mother and added, "She gives me heck about it all the time. According to Mom, I look like a call girl. But then, I suppose that's Bill's intent."

Jordan glanced at the front seat. Luckily, her kids were oblivious to the conversation. "What do you tell them?"

Almost immediately her expression turned carefully blank. She adjusted the quilt over her mother's shoulder, refusing to meet his gaze. "That I have to work. That I'm a dancer. They've seen *Muppets On Ice* and think it's something like that."

She shrugged and Jordan suddenly realized she was still wearing only his coat over a very revealing, enticing costume. He wanted to curse his own stupidity. Why the hell hadn't he thought to grab her some decent clothes before they'd left the house? Everyone in the hospital would be staring at her.

As if she'd read his thoughts, she said, "It doesn't

matter." She leaned over her mother, saw that her eyes were open and alert and smiled. "Does it, Mom?"

The older woman tried for her own smile beneath the oxygen mask, and gave one slight, negative shake of her head.

Georgia sighed. "What am I going to do with you, Mom? You're just too darn good to me."

Her mother gave her a ferocious frown, and Georgia's eyes filled with new tears. She laughed to cover them up. "No, don't yell at me. Just save your breath."

Jordan couldn't bear to see her pain. "It'll be all right, Georgia."

"Yes, of course it will." She looked up at him. "I just thought of something. You two haven't been introduced. Mom, this is Jordan Sommerville, White Knight extraordinaire. And that hulk driving—don't know if you got a good look at him, but he *is* a hulk—he's Morgan Hudson, Jordan's half brother and the sheriff of Buckhorn. Jordan, this is Ruth Samson."

Jordan nodded his head formally. "Glad to make your acquaintance, Ms. Samson." He didn't bother to tell Georgia that she needn't have explained his relationship to Morgan quite so precisely. They'd all been raised together, and were as close as any full-blooded brothers could be.

"Speaking of brothers," Morgan said from the front seat as he handed a cell phone over his shoulder to Jordan, "call Gabe and tell him to go sit on Malone. I don't want her up running around."

Jordan took the phone, and then noticed the look of guilt on Georgia's face. Their eyes met and she winced.

"I'm sorry you got pulled away from your wife, sheriff."

Morgan blared his sirens for a second as he rolled through a red light, alerting any traffic and making the kids squeal. He said to Georgia, "Don't worry about it. Gabe can handle things. And Malone will understand. She's stubborn, but she has an enormous heart."

"He's madly in love," Jordan said dryly, explaining away his brother's description of his wife. He dialed the phone and Gabe immediately answered. Jordan skipped the niceties and asked, "Who's with Misty?"

"Lizzy's looking after her," Gabe said, then: "We've been waiting to hear from you."

Jordan covered the phone and said to Morgan, "Elizabeth's with her."

"Not good enough. Malone can bulldoze her. Tell Gabe to go."

Jordan rolled his eyes. "Morgan wants you to go sit on Misty and make certain she stays in bed."

"I will. But do you need anything? Misty said you were brawling at a bar or something."

There was an undertone of laughter in his youngest brother's voice. "No, I was not brawling."

He'd thought Georgia was distracted, but at his words, one slim brow went up. Jordan shook his head and explained as briefly as possible what they were doing. "We'll be at the hospital in just a few minutes."

Gabe whistled low. "Damn. You want me to send Casey over there? He just got home from a date. His car is still warm."

Jordan thought about it for two seconds. "Yeah, that might not be a bad idea." He eyed Georgia's mostly naked legs and exposed cleavage. Turning slightly away from her, he muttered, "Have Casey bring a change of clothes, okay? From one of the women." Then he rethought that and added, "Make it a big shirt, maybe one of yours or Sawyer's."

"Chesty, is she?"

"Yeah."

Through an undertone of laughter, Gabe said, "I'll see what I can do."

"Thanks. I imagine we'll be at the hospital for a spell, and I know Morgan would like to head home."

Morgan heard him and said, "Hey, I'm in no rush." But Jordan knew that he was, that he wanted to be with Misty and Amber. A more doting father and husband had never been created.

"Will do," Gabe said. "Tell Morgan not to worry— and if you need me just give a buzz."

"Thanks, Gabe." He closed the phone and turned to Georgia as Morgan pulled into the hospital lot.

She tilted her head. "Another brother?"

"The youngest, and most recently married. With only one anniversary to his credit, Gabe still considers himself a newlywed. He's sending my nephew, Casey, here. I hope you don't mind, but I thought he could bring you—"

"Clothes. I heard."

She hadn't quite looked at him and it frustrated him. "Look, Georgia, I don't mean to criticize exactly—"

She interrupted his awkward explanation. "Believe me, I'll be grateful to get into something different." She glanced down at her own breasts and made a sound of disgust. "I don't wear this stuff by choice."

Jordan nodded, uncertain what he could say to that.

She looked hot enough to tempt a saint, and he supposed that was the main reason for wearing the outfit on stage.

To his surprise, she said, "Thanks for thinking of it."

"No problem." With her sitting so close to him, and having so much skin exposed, it was a wonder he'd been able to think of anything else. "Unfortunately, it'll take Case a little while to get here."

Morgan pulled right up to the emergency entrance, and what with his flashing lights and the earlier call, it only took about fifteen seconds before a stretcher was rolled out to the Bronco and Ruth was being taken inside.

Georgia looked overwhelmed by the speed at which things were happening. She rushed to get her kids out of the car, trying to reassure them and keep sight of her mother as she was being whisked away.

Jordan touched her arm as she started to lift Adam from the front seat. "Go on, Georgia." She glanced up at him, clearly distracted. "Get your mother settled and appease the hospital officials with all the paperwork they'll need. The kids and I will meet you in the waiting room when you're done."

She looked at him as though he was insane, cuddling her children closer in a protective gesture and attempting to walk around him. Jordan moved to her side and kept pace with her hurried stride. Both kids stumbled along while staring up at him.

Just as the automatic entry doors opened with a swoosh, he heard Morgan call out that he'd park and be right in. Jordan waved him off.

"Georgia..."

Her high heels clicked on the tiled floor. "Come on, kids. We have to hurry."

There was a note of brittle urgency in her voice that tortured him. No woman should ever be put in such a position. Jordan again took her arm, this time pulling her to a stop. The children seemed fascinated. "Georgia, listen to me."

Utter exasperation, exhaustion, and near panic filled her face. *"What?"*

Well aware of the kids' engrossed attention, and at how close Georgia was to losing it, Jordan spoke softly, giving her a very direct look. "You can trust me, sweetheart. I swear it."

She shook her head, her face pale.

"We'll be in the waiting room," he added, ignoring her refusal, "just around the corner, drinking hot chocolate and watching television and talking." He reached out for Lisa's hand, praying she wouldn't shy away from him, and let out a breath when she released her mother and moved to his side. Her shy smile showed one missing front tooth.

Jordan enclosed her tiny hand in his own. To Georgia, he said, "Did I tell you my oldest brother is a doctor? Well he is. Everyone at the hospital knows Sawyer, though he's always chosen to work from home, treating the people of Buckhorn. He has an office at the back of the house. His son, Casey, is the one who's bringing you some clothes."

She looked around and bit her lip when she saw her mother being wheeled beyond a thick white door. A nurse stood there, papers in hand, waiting for Georgia.

Jordan felt something against his side and looked

down. Adam, chewing on the edge of his coat collar and staring up with big brown eyes, leaned trustingly against Jordan's thigh. His heart swelled with an indefinable affection. He put his hand on the boy's downy head and said again, "You can trust me, Georgia."

She wavered, probably aware she had few choices, then dropped to her knees. Pulling the coat collar from Adam's mouth, she said, "If you have to use the bathroom, or get hungry, tell Mr. Sommerville, okay?"

Adam nodded, then gave her a huge hug. Lisa was next. "We'll drink hot chocolate," she said, mimicking Jordan.

Georgia's smile was misty. "Okay, sweetie, but not too much. It'll keep you awake."

Adam tilted his head. "But we can't sleep here, huh?"

"Sure you can." Georgia grinned, kissed him again, then stood. "There's probably a nice soft couch for you to get comfy on. If you get tired, just close your eyes and pretend you're at home. And before you know it, I'll be right back."

Jordan watched her stride quickly to the desk, her legs looking absurdly long in the high heels. Her shoulders were stiff beneath his jacket, her hands fisted on the strap of her purse. Every line of her body bespoke tension and exhaustion and fear.

A nurse, repeatedly looking Georgia over in her sexy costume, waited for her behind the desk. After Georgia had seated herself and began digging through her purse, no doubt hunting up an insurance card for her mother, Jordan looked down at the kids. Adam raised his arms and, without thinking about it,

Jordan lifted the boy. He was stocky, more compact than his sister who looked almost fey she was so slight. Small arms wrapped around his neck.

"Hot chocolate," Adam said, trying for an adolescent dose of subtlety, "sure sounds good." Jordan bit back a smile. It didn't make any sense and he knew he must be losing his mind, but despite all the chaos, despite the horrid situation and his worry for Georgia and his disapproval of where she worked, he felt good, from the inside out.

Probably better than he had in months.

Oh, hell.

4

CASEY PULLED IN the hospital parking lot and turned off the engine. He'd driven his father's car, a spacious sedan, rather than the truck he usually favored. As he understood it, Jordan was with a woman and her two children—too many people to fit into the truck. He was anxious to hear what story his uncle Jordan told to explain all this.

But for the moment he was more concerned with how to handle Emma Clark.

The truck, being a stick shift, would have guaranteed some space between them. But the car had bench seats, and Emma scooted much too close. She smelled nice, damp from the outdoors and sweet like a female. He was far from immune. She reached for his knee before he could open his door.

"Just a second, Case." Her voice was low, throaty. "Why're you in such a hurry?"

Very calmly, Casey took her wrist and lifted her hand away. She was the most brazen girl he knew, and the most insecure. It was something in her big brown eyes, something she tried real hard to hide.

Twining his fingers with hers, he couldn't help but notice how small boned she was, how her hand felt tiny in his own. "It's almost one in the morning, Emma." The parking lot was well lit, sending slashes of light across her features, making her eyes look even bigger than usual. "What were you doing out on the road alone?"

She rolled one shoulder beneath the shirt he'd insisted she put on. He'd been left in nothing more than an undershirt, but that was better than seeing her traipse around half-naked. He still couldn't believe she'd been moseying down the damn highway so late, wearing her short white shorts, sandals, and a hot-pink halter top that left more bare than it covered. He'd recognized her world-class behind the moment his headlights had hit her. Of course he'd offered her a ride.

Of course she'd accepted. Emma had been after him for months.

"A shrug is not an answer, Em."

She shrugged again, smiling at him and flipping her bleached-blond hair behind her. Casey assumed her natural hair color was a dark brown, judging by her brows and thick lashes. Although that could be makeup, too. She wore a lot of it. She looked...brassy. Almost cheap. And though he had no intention of telling her so, she made him sweat.

"I got mad at my date," she said in her low drawl, "so I took off." Her mouth, shiny with lip gloss that a few of the guys had told him tasted like cherries, tilted up at the corners. "Why d'you care?"

Casey snorted at that lame explanation and defensive response, deciding not to question her further. At seventeen, Emma's idea of a date was to be picked up long enough to add to her already questionable reputation, then get dropped off again. He'd never understand her, but he couldn't help feeling sorry for her.

Just as he couldn't help wanting her.

"C'mon. I need to get inside." When he got out of the car, she scrambled out, too, and rushed around to him.

"You're not mad at me, are you?"

He pulled the bag of clothes from the back seat, sparing her a quick glance. "It's really none of my business, Emma."

She looked hurt for a moment, then the shirt slid off her shoulder and his gaze dropped to her scantily covered chest. He turned abruptly away.

She ran to keep up with him as he headed inside. Thankfully it had stopped raining, but the air felt too cool and still too damp. Water dripped from every tree, shrub and building. He felt a bit chilled. Or at least he had moments ago, before he'd noticed that the night air had caused her nipples to tighten.

He wouldn't look at her there again.

Once inside, he made his way to the waiting room, where he assumed he'd find his uncles. His stride was long, a little too fast, but a small smile curled his mouth as he remembered Gabe relaying the evening's events. His uncle Jordan in a fight? It sounded absurd, although he'd grown up hearing stories of the few occasions when Jordan had lost it, giving into his fierce temper. It wasn't something Casey had ever seen, but he'd believed it was possible.

Jordan was just so...intense. Especially about things he really believed in.

Or people he cared about.

Casey rounded the corner to the open waiting area and stopped short at the sight of Jordan with a little boy sound asleep in his lap. There was a chocolate mustache on the kid, and he was snoring softly. Casey grinned. Jordan had a poleaxed expression on his face, as if deep in thought.

Morgan sat on the floor opposite a tiny girl with a glass-topped coffee table between them, playing Go Fish. Casey had stopped so abruptly, Emma bumped into his back. His breath caught as he felt her soft, young body flush against his. Her hands settled low on his hips and she went on tiptoe, her warm lips touching his ear as she whispered, "Sorry."

Casey ignored her.

"Have I missed anything important?"

Jordan glanced up, then raised one finger to his mouth, cautioning Casey to be quiet. Carefully, his movements very slow, Jordan removed the bundle from his lap and put the boy on the couch. He covered him with his coat. With a wide yawn and a little squirreling around, the kid resettled himself into a rolled-up lump and dozed off again.

Morgan laid his cards down and pushed to his feet. "'Bout time you got here." He nodded to the little girl. "Lisa here is a card shark."

Lisa—long brown hair in disheveled braids—grinned at what she obviously considered a compliment. Morgan tugged on one of those braids with affection. "Maybe she'll be gentler with you, Casey."

Casey leaned in the wide door frame. "I dunno. She's got that ruthless look about her."

Lisa looked up at him, blinked, and kept on looking. Like a natural-born flirt, she batted her long eyelashes at Casey and gave him a wide, adoring grin. She even sighed.

Morgan turned to Jordan. "Would you look at that? She's only six and even she's smitten by him."

Jordan grunted. "He's worse than Gabe."

"Or better."

Casey laughed out loud, well used to their razzing. "Kids just like me."

Morgan looked at him from under his brows. "Females just like you, you mean."

Casey shrugged. It was true, as far as it went. The females did seem to like him. Since he'd first become a teenager, they'd been after him. Not that he had any intentions of getting permanently caught.

Morgan glanced around the waiting room. It looked like chaos with empty foam cups and candy wrappers and kids shoes on the floor. "You okay here now," he asked Jordan, "or do you want me to stick around?"

Jordan stretched tiredly. "We're fine. Go on home. You're starting to get worry lines."

Case walked the rest of the way into the room, keeping his voice as low as his uncles'. "And here I thought those were laugh lines caused by his sunny disposition." Morgan swatted at Casey, making him duck. "Gabe told me to tell you that Misty is sound asleep, konked out from the medicine Sawyer gave her, so you don't have to keep fretting."

Morgan's shoulders—wide as an ax handle—softened with relief. "And Amber?"

Thoughts of his little cousin, now nearing the terrible twos, which on her weren't so terrible, made Casey chuckle. "She wore herself out chasing Gabe in a pillow fight. Last I saw her, she was as zonked as the little guy there." He indicated the boy on the couch.

Jordan rubbed his chin, appearing somewhat exhausted and ultimately pleased at the same time. It was a strange expression for him. "That's Adam, Georgia's son."

"Georgia?"

Morgan leaned forward and said in a whisper, "The bar dancer who Jordan fought over."

"I did *not* fight over her."

"Shh!" Morgan gave him a severe frown for his raised voice.

Jordan glanced at Lisa, who was oblivious as she attempted to shuffle the cards, which sent them all flying to the floor. "It was a misunderstanding," he growled in a lowered voice.

Casey noticed his uncle's color was a bit high and choked back a grin. "Hey, whatever you say, Jordan."

Morgan shook his head, then looked beyond Casey with a questioning frown. Casey turned and saw that Emma had backed up until she was against the wall beside a plastic floor plant. It almost seemed she was trying to be invisible, which of course was impossible for a girl who looked like Emma.

He frowned. So brazen one minute—especially when they were alone—and so timid the next.

He held out his hand. "Emma, have you met my uncles?"

Her big brown eyes widened at the attention given to her, and she swallowed hard. For the first time that Casey could ever remember, her face turned bright red. "I've...um, that is, I know who they are of course, but we've never actually been introduced or anything."

Since Casey still stood there with his hand out, she

finally stepped forward and took it, the embarrassed heat positively pulsing in her cheeks.

He rubbed her knuckles with his thumb, trying to reassure her. Damned if he knew why. "Emma, my uncle Jordan and my uncle Morgan."

Strangely enough, she did an awkward curtsy of sorts, then looked appalled at herself. "Uh,...hi."

Morgan grinned, which always made him look menacing. "You two out on a late date?"

"No." Casey turned her loose so fast, both his uncles scowled at him. He hadn't meant to hold her hand anyway. "I just picked her up."

Jordan raised both brows at that.

Emma pulled the shirt tight around her and folded her arms beneath her breasts. "Casey is just...giving me a ride. Home, I mean."

"But you live in Buckhorn," Morgan pointed out. "Isn't that right?"

"Yeah." Even her neck turned red. "I was...um, headed that way, but Casey said he needed to come here first, then he'd drop me off later."

Morgan glanced at Casey, then back at Emma. "If you're in a hurry to get home, I can drop you off on my way. I'm heading out now."

Jordan made a disgusted sound and stepped in front of Morgan. Casey knew he was trying to shield Emma, since Morgan tended to always look a bit like a marauder. "You and Casey can both head out. I think they'll probably get Georgia's mother settled in her own room soon."

Emma glanced at Casey. He took his time thinking about it, not wanting to embarrass her, but not wanting to give her the wrong impression either. "You want to call your folks first, so they won't be worrying?"

"No."

She said that far too quickly and Jordan and Morgan shared a look. It didn't surprise Casey; he'd already figured out Emma's home life wasn't exactly ideal. If it had been, no way would she have been walking home alone at this time of night. Or done half the other things her reputation suggested. He turned back to his uncles.

"You're sure you don't want me to stick around, Jordan?"

Jordan gave Casey a searching look before he shook his head. "We'll be fine."

As Casey handed him the keys to the car, Morgan took Jordan's arm. "I want to talk to Jordan for just a minute, Case. Can you keep an eye on the kids?"

Lisa looked up and sighed at him again. Casey smiled. "No problem."

"Thanks. I'll bring the Bronco around and wait out front for you both."

THEY WERE barely around the corner when Morgan asked, "What the hell is Casey doing out so late with that girl?"

Jordan shrugged. "Hell if I know. But I don't think there's anything going on between them."

"Why not?"

"She doesn't look like his usual type."

Morgan snorted. "Like Georgia is your usual type?"

Jordan almost faltered. He did frown. "Who says I'm even interested?"

Morgan came to a complete stop and turned to give

Jordan an incredulous look. "Well, let's see. You can't
look at her without tensing up. And that hard-on you
had while arguing with her might be a good clue."

Jordan flushed. And it made him madder than hell,
because not a single one of his other damned brothers
would have. They'd have grinned, hell, they might've
even bragged. They would not, however, have turned
red. But Jordan wasn't at all pleased that all he had to
do was breathe in Georgia's scent and he wanted her.
Bad.

Morgan shook his head. "It's a full moon tonight,
did you know that? Maybe that accounts for a few
things. Like Casey showing up with a girl that I know
damn good and well has a reputation that far exceeds
the one Gabe had at her age. And that's saying something."

"Are you sure about that?" Jordan frowned, concern for his nephew overshadowing his embarrassment. And talking about Casey was definitely prefer-
able to talking about himself. Or Georgia. Or him and
Georgia.

"Yeah. It's a long sad story and I'm too damn tired
to go into it tonight. Besides, I reckon Casey has a handle on things. Though she's not eighteen yet, so if you
get the chance, warn him to be careful, okay?"

Jordan nodded. While Casey was only eighteen
himself, he gave the impression of being much, much
older.

"At least it's stopped raining." The doors slid open
as Morgan approached them. He looked outside, giving Jordan his back as he surveyed the starless sky.
With a nonchalance that didn't fool Jordan for a min-

ute, Morgan asked, "Should we expect you back at the house tonight?"

Jordan hadn't really thought about it, but now that he did... He dropped his head forward, brooding. His muscles felt tight and he rolled his shoulders, trying to relieve some of the tension.

But there was no hope for it. "She doesn't have a car," he said, stating an obvious fact. "Hers is still at the bar."

Morgan nodded. "I know."

"It doesn't seem right to leave her and two kids at a house alone, with no transportation. What if something happened? What if she no sooner got home and her mother needed her?"

"And odds are," Morgan interjected, going right along with him, "even if her mother rests easy tonight, Georgia'll still want to check on her first thing in the morning, so she'll probably need a ride. Assuming you all get to go home tonight at all." Morgan faced him again. "I can't see you leaving her here alone."

"No, I wouldn't do that." Jordan gestured at the mostly quiet hospital. "With the kids and everything...."

"Yeah." Morgan tilted his head, his expression thoughtful. "So I guess we'll see ya sometime in the morning." He stepped into the open doorway. "Let me know tomorrow if there's something I can do to help."

"Thanks."

"Oh, and Jordan?"

Wishing his damn brother would just go away, Jordan raised a brow. "What?"

Morgan grinned. "It's going to get worse before it gets better. I just thought I should let you know that."

Jordan stiffened. "You don't know what the hell you're talking about."

"On the contrary, I married Malone, didn't I? I know exactly what I'm talking about. And my advice would be not to fight it."

"It?"

"The whole chemistry thing."

"Oh, for the love of—"

Morgan shrugged. "You should just give up right now, and save yourself a pound of heartache. Tell her what it is you want. Be up front with her."

Tell her that he wanted to strip her naked? That he wanted to bury himself inside her and spend all night finding ways to make her climax—and the fact that she was a mother, that she danced for drunks, that she didn't appear to particularly like him, hadn't blunted his need one bit? "She has two children, Morgan."

"So? She's still sexy as hell. Any man who's seen her in that getup she's wearing tonight can damn sure vouch for that. Besides, the more you fight it, the worse it is. You're caught. You might as well accept it."

Morgan walked away before Jordan could correct him, before he could assure him that he wasn't *caught* at all! He was turned on, to where he couldn't seem to stop shaking, to stop wanting.

But that was all it was.

Hell, Morgan had taken one look at Misty Malone and started acting the fool. He'd fallen head over ass for her in a single heartbeat.

But he wasn't Morgan. Just as he wasn't Sawyer or

Gabe. He wasn't looking for a wife, had no desire for home and hearth, and even if he was, Georgia wouldn't qualify as wifely material. Not for him.

Still, maybe Morgan was right. What did he have to lose if he told her flat out that he wanted her? She had reacted to him, he wasn't imagining that. Maybe that chemistry mumbo jumbo had some truth to it. Maybe she wouldn't mind an uninvolved sexual relationship.

Jordan swallowed hard at the mere thought, imagining her saying yes, imagining her peeling off that skimpy costume for him....

Oh, hell. *Her outfit.* If she came back to the waiting room before Jordan could head her off and give her the change of clothes, who knew how Casey might react. There was no doubt he'd be surprised, because who would expect a woman to be running around a hospital dressed as she was?

He didn't want Casey to accidentally hurt her feelings with his shock. And he didn't want his nephew ogling her either.

Unfortunately, Jordan reached the waiting room just in time to see Georgia stumble over her own feet. She stared toward Casey, who'd stood when she entered the room.

"Who," Georgia asked, eyeing the way her daughter clung to Casey's hand, "are you?"

"He's Casey," Lisa said.

Casey smoothed his dark blond hair out of his eyes, then held out his free hand. "I gather you're Lisa's mother?"

Georgia looked mesmerized, then gave him her hand. She tipped her head back to see Casey's face, before looking him over with awe. "Why, I wonder, did I think you'd look like an average kid?"

Casey grinned, showing off his killer smile and shaking her hand gently. "I don't know, ma'am."

"Is the whole family like you?"

Emma, who had been sitting quietly on the couch by Adam's feet, spoke up. "Yes, they are."

"Incredible."

Jordan stepped up behind her. "Casey brought you a change of clothes."

"Oh, yeah." Casey reached for the bag and offered it to her. "Honey, my stepmother, wasn't sure what size you might be, so she told me to apologize and explain that she sent things that would adjust." To Jordan, he said, "She refused to send her a man's shirt."

Georgia looked into the bag and pulled out white, elastic waist cotton slacks, a soft pink cotton T-shirt, and a long sleeved matching cardigan. There was even a pair of slip-on casual canvas shoes.

She glanced back up at Casey with a grateful smile. "Please be sure to tell her how much I appreciate this. And I promise to return the clothes right away."

Casey skipped a look toward Jordan before smiling. "You can tell her yourself. She said to invite you and your family over to the big cookout at the end of the month. Honey likes to show all our neighbors how much she appreciates them by having this huge get-together. It worked out real well last year, so she wants to make it a traditional gathering."

Jordan choked and considered stuffing Casey into the damn bag. Georgia, he noticed, looked panicked.

"But..." She sputtered, her gray eyes wide, "We're not neighbors!"

"You live in Buckhorn?"

Georgia nodded.

"Close enough." He ignored Jordan when he added, "You don't have to wait till then to visit though. Our house is pretty far off the main road without any other houses close by. Honey said to tell you she'd love the company anytime you feel up to visiting."

Lisa clapped her hands together, staring with naked adoration toward Casey. "Can we, Mommy, please, please, please?"

"But..."

Casey ruffled Lisa's hair, then turned to the couch, caught Emma's hand and pulled her to her feet. She tried to hang onto his hand, but Casey made that impossible. "We've got to go before Morgan leaves without us."

Georgia hustled after him. "Wait! Please, tell your stepmother—"

"Honey."

"Yes, well, tell Honey that I appreciate the offer, but I can't possibly come."

"Jordan'll bring you." Casey stared at Jordan, knowing exactly what he was doing. His brown eyes warmed to glittering amber as he said, "He wouldn't want to disappoint Honey."

Keeping a relationship purely sexual, Jordan thought, would be pretty damn tough if the whole family got to know her. But then he looked at Lisa, and he gave up with a sound somewhere between a growl and a sigh. "No, I don't want to disappoint Honey."

Georgia held the clothes clutched to her spectacular

chest, her pale gray eyes flared with dismay, her golden brown hair practically standing on end.

And perversely, Jordan said, "I insist. It'll be fun."

"But..."

He turned away and bid Casey and Emma goodnight, noticing that Casey was staying just out of Emma's reach. He shook his head.

"What?"

Georgia stood beside him. He could smell her, warm and sweet, and he wanted to press his nose into her neck, taste her skin. "My nephew," he said in a rough voice, filled with lust, though she didn't seem to know it, "didn't even notice what you're wearing."

He hadn't quite realized it until he said it. But not once did Casey look her over. He'd kept his gaze respectfully on her face, his manner as polite and friendly as ever.

Georgia looked down at herself. "I know you think I should be embarrassed." She met his gaze, her eyes now somber, sad. "But I'm just too worried."

Jordan touched her cheek. That didn't seem like enough so he put his arm around her shoulders and led her to the chair Casey had just vacated. Luckily, there was no one else in this particular waiting room. Earlier a man had come in with a badly cut finger, and a woman had shown up with a twisted ankle. But they had each been attended to and no one had shown up since.

Once Georgia was seated, her hands twisting in the clothing Honey had sent, Jordan asked, "What did they say about your mother? How is she?"

He knelt in front of her, unable to stop touching her. This time his hands rested on her knees. Her skin was so incredibly warm, so silky, he wanted to part her thighs, wanted to tip up her face and kiss her deeply as he moved between her legs. Her thighs were strong, he'd seen that as she danced, and he could only imagine how tightly she'd hold him.

She didn't seem to notice his touch or his preoccupation, or else she didn't care.

Jordan shook himself. Adam snored nearby on the couch and Lisa was starting to get bored with the cards. She'd taken to deliberately scattering them, and the last time they'd flown everywhere, she hadn't bothered to pick them back up.

He had to get hold of himself. Lusting after a woman in front of her children wasn't something he ever would have done. He wouldn't do it now. Out of all the brothers, he was the one most circumspect, most discerning.

"Will she be all right, Georgia?"

Georgia nodded. "Mom has emphysema. My father was a big cigar smoker and they say it was his second-hand smoke that..." She looked furious for a moment, then started over. "She's never been a smoker herself. In fact she hates the things."

"Me, too." He took one of her hands, and she didn't pull away.

"They think she has bronchitis. With her lung disease, that's a big problem. They're going to keep her a few days, put her on IV antibiotics, do a breathing treatment every four hours or so. As soon as they get her settled in her room and I make sure she's got everything she needs, I'll be able to head home. I just don't want to go until I know—"

"Of course not. There's no rush."

She gave him a distracted, grateful nod.

"When was the last time you ate?"

She looked at him as if he were crazy. "I'm not hungry. But the kids..." She glanced over at the couch. Jordan looked, too. Lisa was still sitting on the floor, but she'd slumped sideways, sound asleep, her head mere inches from her brother's big toe.

Jordan grinned. "I fed them. It wasn't the most nutritional meal going. Just sub sandwiches from the vending machine with chips and hot chocolate."

She rubbed her forehead with a shaking hand. "I should have thought of it. Thank you. It didn't even occur to me..."

"Hey." Jordan leaned lower to see her averted face. Very gently he touched her chin. "You had your hands full."

"I'll pay you back. How much was it?"

Her polite query set his teeth on edge. "I don't want your money, Georgia."

To his surprise, she came to her feet, making him quickly stand so he wouldn't be stampeded. "It's not your job to take care of my children."

Jordan crossed his arms over his chest and stared down at her, studying her set expression. "I don't mind helping out."

Her soft lips flattened into a hard line. The way she squeezed Honey's clothes, they'd be all wrinkled by the time she got them on. Not that he was in any hurry for her to change now that they were virtually alone. The kids were asleep, Casey and Morgan had left, the hospital was quiet.

She looked incredible, sexy and tousled and earthy.

His breath came a little faster. "You're going to need more help, you know."

She rounded on him, nearly dropping the clothes. Her eyes, circled with smeared mascara and exhaustion, turned stormy gray. She kept her voice low, but it sounded like a growl. "We'll manage just fine."

"Georgia..."

Her chin lifted. "You can leave now. I'm sorry I kept you so long. I lost track of the time, but now that I know my mother will be all right, I can—"

Very gently, he interrupted her. "You know I'm not going to leave."

"Don't be ridiculous. It's..." She looked around for a clock.

"It's very late." Jordan kept his tone soft and easy, soothing her. He had no idea why she'd suddenly turned defensive, except that she probably hadn't eaten for a while, her mother was sick, and she'd nearly been arrested.

And he couldn't stop thinking about getting her naked and under him. Or over him. Or...

He felt like a complete bastard. "Listen to me, Georgia." He waited until her eyes lifted to his. "I'm going to drive you home after everything is taken care of here."

"*Why?*" She stared at him, her face flushed. "You don't even know me. And what you do know about me, you disapprove of. You certainly don't owe me anything."

"Georgia." He said her name like a caress. He didn't mean to, but he did. "No man would leave you here alone like this."

She laughed at that, a mean, bitter laugh. "You are so wrong."

It took a lot of effort not to get riled, not to react to his sudden suspicions. But she was too upset right now, too overwhelmed, for him to start interrogating her. There'd be plenty of time for him to learn more about her past later. He'd see to that. "How else would you get home?"

"We can take a cab." She drew a shuddering breath. "Since I got my money from Bill, I can easily afford—"

Jordan took her shoulders and pulled her closer to him, leaning down so that he could whisper. The very last thing he wanted to do was wake the children.

Her eyelashes fluttered at his nearness, but she didn't look into his eyes. She stared at his mouth instead.

"I'm taking you home, Georgia. Accept it. We'll get your car tomorrow and then you can check on your mother and, after all that, we'll talk about the cookout my family has planned."

She covered her ears with her hands and pulled away. "I have to change now. Will you..." She made a disgusted sound. "Will you stay here with Lisa and Adam?"

"Of course." Why was she covering her ears? It wasn't like he'd been being abusive. He'd offered her help. He'd been gentle, calm. He hadn't told her that he wanted her, that just touching her damn shoulders and bringing her close had nearly driven him to his knees and made him semierect.

He watched her walk away, and decided that he *would* tell her. Tonight.

He wasn't at all sure he could last another day this way.

5

THE CAR RIDE home was mostly silent. There wasn't a single other vehicle on the road, the kids were sound asleep and the clouds had finally cleared enough to let the moonlight dance over the wet streets. Overall, it was a sleepy, relaxing, lulling ride.

But she was far from relaxed. "Jordan...I'm sorry I lost my temper with you."

Jordan glanced at her as if surprised that she'd spoken. Aside from getting her arrested, he'd been wonderful, and she'd been a raving bitch. All because he scared her.

And when she was around him, she scared herself. The man didn't need to say anything important, not even anything seductive, and she wanted him. An intolerable situation, and she was far too tired to deal with it.

She could hear the smile in his mellow, mesmeric voice when he spoke. "No problem. You've had a rough day."

Georgia made a sound of agreement, leaned her head back and closed her eyes. Maybe if she didn't look at him, if she didn't see his wide, hard shoulders, the thickness of his muscled forearms, the way his light brown hair caught the moonlight and how deep, how seductive his green eyes were when he turned them toward her—well, maybe it would help. But she doubted it. He was a sinfully gorgeous male, tall and strong and hard, but she'd seen strong attractive men before, dealt with them every night at the bar. No, it was much more than Jordan's looks, much more than his physical attributes.

All the man had to do was mutter two syllables and she wanted to melt. Something about his voice affected her deep down inside, stripping away her defenses. It made her imagine awful, wonderful things.

She shook her head, more at herself than anything he did or said. "I appreciate the ride home. And how you carried the kids out. I could have managed, but—"

"But you've had enough to deal with." He reached across the seat and his large hand squeezed her shoulder. Even through the borrowed T-shirt, his touch was electric. She caught her breath, not wanting him to know how he affected her, how amazingly turned on she was even at this moment.

She'd had very little sleep over the past two days. She'd worked a double shift and dealt with the threat of being arrested, then the gut-wrenching fear over her mother's health. She had no idea how she was going to manage to work and take care of her mother at the hospital, with no baby-sitter. Things looked very grim.

But still she wanted him when she never wanted any guy. She'd long since considered herself immune to the normal urges most women felt. So what if Jordan was an uncommonly patient and wonderful man? She shouldn't care that he was gorgeous and as finely built as a Greek statue, or that he had a voice warm enough to melt butter.

She knew he disapproved of her, and that should have taken care of the rest. But somehow, maybe because her children seemed so taken by him, his disapproval didn't matter.

"You deserve to take a break, Georgia. And I like your kids. Adam reminds me a little of Casey when he was that age. Constant motion right up until he runs out of steam."

A distracting topic if ever there was one. She gladly accepted it. "Your nephew certainly took me by surprise."

Jordan's smile was gentle and filled with pride. "He's an amazing kid. Only eighteen, but I swear he has more common sense, more backbone and maturity than a lot of men twice his age. We pretty much raised him ourselves, you know."

She didn't know. Since she'd moved to Buckhorn, she'd kept to herself except for her work. And she certainly hadn't tried to form any friendships at the bar. She didn't have time to gossip with neighbors, or go out of her way to get to know anyone. "We, meaning you and your brothers?"

"That's right. Casey's mother couldn't deal with a newborn infant, and she took off. Sawyer, my oldest brother, the one who's a doctor? He was still in medical school when Case was born, but he brought him home from the hospital and that was that. I was...let's see, fifteen at the time. And I remember being absolutely fascinated. I looked up to Sawyer and Morgan a lot, and I'd always seen them in a one dimensional way, you know?"

"Yes." She saw most men in a one dimensional way—*selfish.* Her father, her ex, her boss, the men who threw money at her while she was on stage.... She squeezed her eyes shut at that thought, praying that none of the men were spending grocery or bill money. Some of them, she was sure, couldn't afford what they tossed at her while downing drink after drink, night after night. And if she thought about that too much, she felt miserably guilty.

But the brothers, even the nephew, had thrown her for a loop. They were unlike any men she'd ever known. Their very posture spoke of confidence and honor and respectability. She found herself intrigued.

Because she knew it had been true for her father, and true for her ex, she asked, "Things changed a lot with a baby in the picture?"

She waited for Jordan's complaints on the hardships of keeping up with an infant. Once again, he took her by surprise.

"I wouldn't say they changed, just adjusted a bit. In a good way. Sawyer was always so straight-faced, so serious. And then there he was, cuddling this little squirt and grinning all the time and looking so happy to change a diaper or give a bath."

Georgia stared at him. When she'd had Lisa, she'd always felt the same way. Everything her baby did she'd thought was magical and amazing. But she'd never considered that a man might have that outlook. "You're serious?"

Nodding, Jordan said, "I used to think nothing could pull Sawyer from his books, not even a beautiful woman. But if Casey made a noise, he was there, checking on him, smiling at him."

Jordan grinned with the memories, then shook his head. "Morgan was always the rowdiest. He fought for the fun of fighting. Everyone still jokes about him bordering on the side of savage."

"I can see that."

Jordan glanced at her quickly before returning his attention to the road. "He makes a hell of an impression, doesn't he? He's kept our town peaceful, usually with little more than a look. But whenever he touched Casey, he was so gentle. It boggled my mind. Now, with his own daughter, Amber, who's heading on two, he's the same. I swear he could wrestle buffalo with one arm and hold her close with the other, making sure not a one of her little curls got ruffled. He makes a hell of a sheriff, and an even better dad."

"You have an impressive family." Beyond impressive really. Having only met Jordan and Morgan, she should have been prepared for Casey. How could he have been anything less than spectacular, surrounded by such incredible uncles?

Jordan gave one nod. "Yeah, I think they're pretty great. Gabe, the youngest, started his own business not too long ago and already he's got more work than he can handle. He can build or repair anything, and after his marriage he decided he needed to get things a little more on track."

"On track how?"

"Before he met Elizabeth, he just worked when the mood struck him—or if someone needed something. He was always willing to help out. But Gabe preferred to spend his time in other pursuits. I doubt there was ever a day when he was without female company. Women flocked to him. It was almost uncanny. From the time he learned the difference between males and females, every girl in the area was after him, and he took advantage of it. They spoiled him rotten."

Jordan said that with a fond smile, making Georgia shake her head.

"The worse his reputation got, the more they seemed to come after him. It used to drive my mother nuts until she and Brett retired to Florida."

His poor wife, Georgia thought. A man like that never settled down, never really gave up his old ways....

Jordan touched her cheek. "Why are you frowning?"

She'd been so absorbed in her thoughts, she hadn't realized she frowned. "No reason."

"Come on, Georgia." He turned down the old road leading to her house. It was bumpy and filled with muddy puddles thanks to the rain. "I could almost see the evil thoughts going through your brain."

"Not evil. Just...realistic."

"Like?"

She didn't appreciate being pushed. She didn't appreciate having him affect her this way, either. Perhaps it would be best to tell him up front exactly how she felt so he'd leave tonight and not come back. That would be the most intelligent course to take.

So then why did the possibility make her feel so desperate?

Georgia cleared her throat, peeked at her kids to make certain they were still sleeping soundly. "Very well. If you're sure you want to hear this?"

"I do."

"I imagine," she said slowly, measuring her words,

"that any man who's used to running from one woman to the next, to indulging every sexual whim, is not likely to settle down with only one woman, just because he says a few vows. If it's in his nature to be a...sexual hedonist—"

Jordan laughed. "Gabe is that."

"—then he'll always be a hedonist."

"True. I won't argue with you there. All of my brothers are very sexual." He glanced at her and shrugged. "There's nothing wrong with that, by the way."

Georgia didn't bother to argue with him on it. She did, however, wonder if he included himself in the "very sexual" category.

No! She did not wonder. She didn't care. Refusing to look at him, she stared out her door window and watched the passing shrubbery on the side of the road. Even in the darkness, everything looked wilted by the rain.

Without her encouragement, Jordan continued. "Gabe is still a man, still very interested in sex, and I can't see that ever changing. But now he does all his overindulging with his wife."

Lord, how had she gotten onto this subject? She felt so hot, her window was beginning to steam. "If you say so," she mumbled, hoping he'd let it go.

But of course he didn't.

"You don't believe me?" When she didn't answer, he whistled. "Must have been a hell of a marriage you had."

Georgia denied that with a shake of her head. "The marriage was fine. It was the end of the marriage that was hell."

So softly she could barely hear him, Jordan asked, "Because you still loved him?"

"No." By the time the divorce was finalized, she knew she'd been living a fairy tale, created and maintained all in the fancy of her mind. She'd seen what she'd wanted to see, not what had really been there. "No, I didn't still love him. And it didn't matter that he had never really loved me. But he never loved his kids, either. And that I can't understand."

"I'm sorry."

"Why?" His voice had that low, hypnotic sound to it again, making her insides tingle, making her breasts feel too full. It pulled at her until she wanted to lean toward him, wanted to press her face into his throat and breathe in his scent, feel the warmth of his hard body. "What difference does it make to you?"

Jordan turned into her driveway and cut the engine. "Maybe I can explain it once we get inside." His gaze, glittering bright, held her. "Go unlock your front door and I'll carry the kids in."

She quickly shook her head, dispelling the trance he'd put her in with that melodic voice. "No. Thank you. You've done enough and I insist on repaying you for your—"

"I'm walking you in, Georgia." His tone was now firm and commanding. His large hand cupped her cheek, tipping up her chin. "We have a few things to say to each other."

"We have nothing to discuss!"

"Mommy?" Lisa sat up, rubbing her eyes and looking around in confusion.

With one last glare at Jordan—where she couldn't help but notice that he appeared understanding and sympathetic still—Georgia got out of the front seat, then opened her daughter's car door. "Sweetheart, we're home." She unfastened Lisa's seat belt and smoothed her tangled bangs out of her face. "Wait right here while I go unlock the door, then I'll get Adam and we'll all go in, okay?"

She'd forgotten to turn on a porch light before they left, and the path to the front door, broken and overgrown with weeds, would have been impossible if Jordan hadn't flipped the headlights back on. Her hand shook as she struggled to get the key into the lock and open the front door. But when she turned around, she almost fell over her daughter.

Jordan stood there, Adam snuggled blissfully unaware in his arms while Lisa held on to one of his belt loops. He gave her a gentle smile and said, "Move."

Like a zombie, Georgia stepped out of the way. What choice did she have? None. As a matter of fact, Jordan, with his quiet, calm ways, had been taking away her choices from the moment she first saw him.

She closed the door and started after him, hearing Lisa direct him to Adam's room at the top of the stairs. Lisa followed him, then veered off to her own bedroom. Georgia went to her first, helping her to get her nightgown on and tucking her into bed.

"I didn't brush my teeth."

Georgia smiled and pressed a kiss to Lisa's forehead. "You'll brush them twice tomorrow morning, okay?"

"Okay. I love you, Mommy."

Tears blurred her eyes for a moment. She was just so tired. And she had so very much to be thankful for.

"Oh baby, I love you, too." She scooped her daughter up for a giant bear hug. "So, so much."

"Will you tell Jordan g'night for me?"

"Of course I—"

"I'm right here." Jordan stepped out of the shadows and sat on the edge of Lisa's bed, practically forcing Georgia to scamper out of his way. He was an enormously large man and took up entirely too much space. "Thanks for helping me out so much today, Lisa. I appreciate it."

Her teeth flashed in a quick smile. "It was fun. Except for grandma gettin' sick."

Jordan stroked her hair. "You were asleep, but your mother assures me that your grandma will be fine. The doctors are going to take very good care of her, and before long, she'll be back home."

Lisa nodded, then looked back at her mother. "Who's going to baby-sit us when you go to work?"

Georgia had been standing there in something of a stupor, amazed and a little appalled at how at ease Jordan seemed to be with her daughter, and how at ease her daughter was with him. There hadn't been many men in their lives, certainly not one who would smooth a blanket and stroke back a wayward curl.

Her father had never been close to her, much less his grandchildren. He'd died without ever knowing how truly wonderful Lisa and Adam were. Her ex-husband had walked away from them without a backward glance. But Jordan Sommerville had not only cared for them, he'd done so willingly, and even claimed to have enjoyed himself.

Seeing him now, she could believe him.

The lump in her throat nearly strangled her. She did

not want to like him, not at all. But it was getting harder to stick to that resolve.

Forestalling her daughter from saying too much, Georgia said, "It's all taken care of, sweetie. I'll tell you about it in the morning. But for now, you need to get to sleep. The sun will be up before you know it."

Just like that, Lisa rolled to her side, snuggled her head into her pillow, and faded back to sleep.

Jordan smiled as he stood. In a low whisper that made every nerve in her body stand on end, he said, "Children are the most amazing creatures. Awake one minute, zonked out the next."

Georgia turned off the bedside lamp, throwing the room into concealing darkness. Only the dim light from the hallway intruded. She headed for the door. "My children are very sound sleepers. Once they're out, not much can wake them."

She turned to pull the door shut and found herself not two inches from Jordan. He looked down at her, his gaze lazy and relaxed. Her heartbeat jumped into double-time. She stared at his mouth—and he moved out of her way.

Georgia decided not to look at him again, but it turned out not to be a worry. He didn't follow her to Adam's room. Instead he headed back downstairs.

She found Adam still in his jeans and T-shirt, but his shoes had been pulled off and the blankets pulled over him. Her heart swelled at the sight of his teddy bear clutched in his arms. How had Jordan known to give it to him? It was a certainty her son hadn't awakened enough to ask for it. But he might have missed it in the middle of night.

She sighed, kissed him gently—which prompted a

snuffled snore—and smiled. She left his room with her thoughts in a jumble, pausing in the hallway for a good three minutes while she tried to figure out how to get rid of Jordan, how to remove him without looking totally ungrateful for all he'd done.

Honesty, she decided, might be her best course. She'd simply tell him outright that she neither wanted nor needed his help—not anymore. She'd thank him for all he'd done that day, regardless of the fact that part of the trouble had been his doing.

Then she'd tell him good-night, and that would be that.

She headed into the kitchen, her back stiff with resolve, and found him making coffee. Before she could speak he turned to her and his expression was so intense, so...sensual, she caught her breath.

"We have to talk," he said, and just those simple words, muttered low and rough, made her heart pound too sharply, her body too warm. She literally trembled with need, and it made her angry and scared and frustrated. How could he affect her this way? He stepped toward her and touched her cheek. "But first, why don't you go get showered and get all this makeup off? The coffee—I found decaf so it won't keep you up—should be done by then."

With her breath coming fast and low, her stomach in knots, Georgia nodded. He was making her coffee, one of her favorite things on this earth. And it sounded heavenly. *He* sounded heavenly. Lord, what a combination.

She hadn't stood a chance.

JORDAN HAD himself well in check. He would stop reacting like a teenager with raging hormones, where the sight of a girl's panties could put him into a frenzy of carnal greed. Hell, he could see a woman *without* her damn panties and still control himself. He would be calm. He would explain to Georgia that he wanted her, that he thought they should take advantage of the incredible chemistry...no, not incredible. Just good old chemistry. Nothing special, but there was no reason why they couldn't get together and, as mature, reasonable adults, have a brief affair.

It only made sense. There was no reason for them *not* to indulge their mutual desire. She was a divorced woman working in a bar. It wasn't like she was a prim and proper virgin.

But even as Jordan listed in his mind all the reasons that they should and could get together to take the edge off the urgent, burning hunger threatening to consume him, he worried that she'd refuse.

Damn, even looking at her sink full of dirty dishes made him want her. The whole house was a wreck, and rather than make him disdainful, it drove home to him how overwhelmed she was. He looked around again and wondered which issue he should resolve first: his lust, or the fact that he was going to give her a helping hand whether she wanted him to or not.

The old house was silent except for the creaking of the pipes as she showered. His hands shook and his vision blurred as he imagined her naked, wet and soapy and slick and...

He groaned aloud. The shower shut off and he pictured her drying her lush breasts, her flat belly, her thighs....

To distract himself, he started on the dishes. She

needed a dishwasher, but there was really no place in the ancient kitchen to put one. The cabinets were a tad warped, some of them mismatched, and they'd been painted many times. They weren't very deep, but there was certainly an abundance of them. Too many, in fact.

The linoleum on the floor, besides being of a singularly ugly design, was cracked and starting to peel. The ceiling, which he guessed to be just beneath the shower judging by the noise, had water stains, indicating that at least a few of those squeaky pipes were leaking.

He was done with the dishes, all of them stacked on a dishtowel to air dry, when the coffee finished dripping. She'd be getting dressed now... Jordan forced himself to keep busy.

Right off the kitchen was a glass-enclosed patio that opened to the backyard. Vents in the floor-to-ceiling windows were opened about an inch, letting in the cool, damp night air. Jordan, who needed a little cooling off, carried his coffee into that room and looked out at the backyard. Beautiful, he thought, even with the rough grounds. There was an enormous oak tree that probably provided an abundance of shade to the room during the hottest part of the day.

A padded glider, two chairs, a few rattan tables that had seen better days, and various toys scattered about filled the room to overflowing.

Light from the kitchen slanted across the floor, mixing with the softer, gentler moonlight. The wind stroked the trees, making the shadows dance. The house, while in need of repair, was perfect. It would take only a few pets—and a man—to make it a complete home.

Jordan held his coffee cup with a barely restrained grip. What was she doing now? How would she dress? He imagined she'd look vastly different in regular clothes, with her hair freshly shampooed and all her overdone makeup gone.

And then finally he heard her.

"Jordan?"

"Right here." The words, whispered low, barely made it past the restriction in his throat. He didn't turn to face her, attempting to get himself back under control first. But damn, it was impossible. It was insane.

He could smell her, he thought with an edge of urgency, sweet and warm and so damn female. Even fresh from her shower, he detected her scent. He felt like a bull in full rut.

He cleared his throat. "There's a cup of coffee waiting for you on the counter."

Her footsteps were nearly silent as she padded to the kitchen and back. He knew she was coming out to him.

"Thank you." She, too, had lowered her voice, and there was an edge of wariness in her tone. He heard her sip, then heard the creak of the glider as she sat down. "I should have known you'd make great coffee."

It sounded like an accusation. Slowly Jordan turned to face her. Moonlight touched her in selective places—over the crown of her hair, making it glow a soft gold, across her shoulders now covered in a baggy white cotton pullover, and her knees, bare from the sloppy gray sweatshorts she wore. There were thick white ankle socks on her feet.

Not a seductive outfit, at least not deliberately. But then, nothing that she'd done to him had been deliberate. Most of her face was hidden, but he saw enough.

"My God, you're beautiful." Without the makeup, she looked young and innocent and...distressed. Because of him?

Her quiet laugh was incredulous. "Hardly that. Only my mother, who loves me dearly, would ever call me beautiful."

Jordan heard the words, but he couldn't quite comprehend them. Not with her sitting there making him shake with the most profound emotions he'd ever experienced.

She laughed again, nervously this time as he continued to stare. "But I suppose anything is an improvement after the war paint, especially since it had all been smudged. I nearly scared myself when I looked in the mirror."

She took another drink of the coffee, then set the mug beside her on the floor. With a loose-limbed dexterity that amazed him, she twisted one leg up across her lap and began massaging her foot. "Now, about our talk."

Jordan looked at her foot, so small and feminine, less than half the size of his own. He breathed hard and felt like an idiot. How the hell could her feet raise his fevered urgency to the breaking point? He searched his beleaguered brain for an ounce of logic.

"You're going to need some help for the next few days." Damn, he hadn't meant to blurt that out.

She paused, looking up at him with a blank sort of disbelief. She forced a smile. "We'll be fine."

In for a penny, in for a pound.... "Who will watch your children," he asked, "while you visit your mother at the hospital? I assume you'll want to visit her?"

That got her frowning. "Of course I will! I'm not going to just leave her there...."

"I didn't think so." The love she felt for her mother, the closeness, was as obvious to him as her feelings for her children. It had pained him to witness her worry, her fear. All his life, he'd had his family around him, his mother, his brothers, ready to share any burdens, ready to support him in any way they could. But the one person Georgia had was now ailing, and it turned him inside out trying to imagine how the hell she could cope with that reality.

His own mother was the epitome of female strength, her love and loyalty unshakeable, unquestionable. She was fierce in her independence, and God help anyone who tried to come between her and her family.

He knew if it was his mother in the hospital right now, he'd move heaven and earth for her. But Georgia didn't have his financial or familial resources.

Georgia needed him, and his mother would be the first to have his head if he didn't insist on helping. As much as it pained him, he was going to have to put lust aside, at least for the time being.

"What will you do when you have to work?" Jordan asked. "Do you have any baby-sitters? Other than your mother, I mean."

Her head snapped up and she dropped her foot

back to the floor. Jordan had a feeling she was ready to pounce on him. He quickly set his own coffee cup on the rickety rattan table and stepped close enough so that she couldn't come completely to her feet without touching him.

He waited, hoping, his breath held. But with no more than a wary look, she retreated.

He settled both hands on her shoulders and gave her his patented stern look. "Is it true, Georgia? Or do you have someone you can call to help out until your mother gets well?"

They were still speaking in hushed tones, and her voice sounded gruff with emotion when she answered. "Of course I have people I can call."

Jordan knelt down in front of her. His long legs encased hers; he surrounded her, wanting her to know he'd protect her, that she could trust him. "Who?"

Silence filled the room. Jordan loved the way her gray eyes darkened, making her thoughts easy for him to read. Others would consider her eyes mysterious, but he understood her. He *knew* her.

Finally, after long seconds, she shook her head.

His heart swelled painfully. "There's no one, is there?" She turned away and he whispered, "Georgia?"

"No."

Without conscious decision, he began caressing her shoulders, feeling the smoothness of her, the softness. In a tone so low he could barely hear himself, he said, "Don't ever lie to me again, Georgia. It's not necessary. Whatever men you've known—"

She laughed at that, a sound without much humor.

"—I'm not like them. You can trust me."

She stared at his mouth. "Oh, I know you're different, Jordan. No doubt about it. But don't you see? That's part of the problem."

"You want to explain that?"

"Why not?" Her hand trembled when she touched his jaw, and her voice was husky with wonder. "I've found it very easy to ignore most men, even the men yelling crude suggestions from the audience when I dance. But I can't ignore you. You make me feel different. You...affect me." Then with a frown: "I don't like it."

For the first time in his life, Jordan's knees felt weak. He sucked in air, trying to fill his lungs enough, trying to dredge up just a little more calm. This was important and he wanted it resolved.

He cupped her face, pulled her forward to the edge of her seat until her breasts were soft and full against his chest, until he could feel her thundering heartbeat, meshing with his own. "You affect me, too."

And then he kissed her.

Her lush mouth softened, warmed, under his. She made a small sound of confusion and her hands settled on his shoulders, her fingers biting deep into his muscles.

He tasted her deeply, his tongue pushing gently into her mouth, making them both groan. Jordan was a hairsbreadth away from taking her completely when he forced himself to lift his mouth away. They both struggled for breath. "This is insane," he whispered.

She nodded, staring into his eyes with a mix of wonder and fear.

"Here's what we're going to do." He used the tone that made women agree with him no matter what. He considered it successful, given that she rested her head on his shoulder and her hands still held him tightly.

"I'll see to the children," he insisted, "after I've taken care of all my appointments. With a little rearranging, I think I can be done by three each day, which means you'll have plenty of time to visit with your mother, and then get into work, right?"

With an obvious effort, she pulled herself away from him. She looked dazed, but said, "Sometimes I waitress in the afternoons, too."

Jordan barely resisted the urge to kiss her again. "You work alternate shifts?"

"No. Sometimes I work both. We...that is, I need the money. This house has a lot of repairs that have to be done and..."

It seemed the words came from her unwillingly. "Shh. I understand. When I can't make it, Casey or one of my other relatives will help out. You'll love them. They're all terrific with kids."

She didn't reply to that, either to deny or accept his offer. Jordan looked at the weariness etched into every line of her body. It was no wonder she looked so tired, so utterly defeated. "You were finishing up a double shift today, weren't you?"

"Yes."

He lifted one hand to her cheek and used his thumb to stroke her cheekbone. "How many hours do you usually work in a day?"

"However many I need to."

Her matter-of-fact answer hit him like a slap. He looked up at the ceiling, wanting to roar with frustration. Since meeting her, he'd been indulging visions of wild lechery while she was barely able to stay on her feet. He felt like a complete and total bastard, an unfeeling—

"What is it you do, Jordan? You said you have appointments?

It wasn't easy to tamp down his anger at the thought of her working herself into the ground, especially at that sorry place. But her exhaustion was a palpable force, wearing her down, *wearing him down*, and he couldn't bring himself to add to it. He reminded himself that she needed his strength, not his temper. Not his lust.

"I'm a vet." He moved to sit beside her on the glider and as she turned toward him, he took her hand. The unusual day had brought them a closeness that might normally have taken a week or more to achieve. He'd seen her vulnerability, and her strength. But they'd had little time to actually get to know one another. He'd rectify as much of that as he could right now.

"I've always loved animals and they've always loved me. I feel gifted, because they respond to me."

"It's your voice," she said, and she smiled.

Jordan shrugged. All his life he'd heard about his mystical voice, but so far, Georgia had seemed quite capable of resisting him. "Why don't you have any pets? The yard is plenty big enough and the kids would love it."

"So would I. But pets cost money. They need food and shots and...not only would it cost too much, but I don't have much spare time left. The kids are too young to be solely responsible for a pet, and my mother does enough as it is."

Jordan decided to think on that. As isolated as she

was in the big house, a dog would be ideal. He said, "I have a clinic not that far from here. That's why it'll be easy for me to help you out with the children. They like me, Georgia, so that shouldn't be a problem. And if you still have any doubts about my character, well, ask around town tomorrow. Anyone can tell you that I'm good baby-sitting material."

She looked down at their clasped hands, then tugged gently until he freed her. Scooting over a little to put some space between them, she again pulled her foot into her lap and began rubbing. In a ridiculously prim voice considering they were sitting alone in the darkness and he'd had his tongue in her mouth only moments before, she said, "I don't want to impose on you."

"I'm offering, and besides—" he tipped her face toward him "—what other options do you have?"

Her eyes closed and she sighed. "Options? I don't have many, do I? I've often wondered what my life would be like with more options."

Jordan growled out a sigh. She was the most exasperating woman he'd ever met. "I'm trying to give you some options, sweetheart."

"Don't call me that."

Jordan ignored her order. "I want you to be able to visit your mother and work without having to worry about Lisa or Adam."

Her eyes slanted his way, heavy with fatigue. "You don't approve of me."

Fighting the urge to shake her, Jordan frowned. "Wrong. I don't approve of where you work. They're two entirely different things."

She laughed at that, and focused on flexing the arch of her left foot with intense concentration.

Jordan caught her wrists. "What are you doing?"

"My feet hurt." Her tone was abrupt, as if that particular question had annoyed her more than anything else. "Try staying on your feet all damn day—in high heels no less—and your feet'll hurt, too."

He flexed his jaw. He told himself to just leave. He even cursed himself privately in the silence of his own mind. But it didn't make one whit of difference. He was already so far off track, he had no idea where he was going, but was just as intent on getting there.

"Lay down."

She reared back as if he'd struck her. *"What?"*

Jordan caught her hips and pulled her toward him so that she landed flat on her back on the flowered cushions. She was stunned for a moment, not moving, and before she could gather her wits he deftly flipped her onto her stomach. He had her feet in his lap and his gaze glued to the sight of her rounded ass in the loose shorts, by the time she started to struggle. He must have masochistic tendencies, he decided, tightening his grip on her ankles, holding her secure.

Georgia levered up on stiffened arms, gasping in outrage—until his fingers moved deeply over the arch of her left foot, then up and over her toes. She gave a long, husky, vibrating groan.

The sound of her unrestrained pleasure made Jordan break out in a sweat. Her shoulders went limp and her head dropped forward as if her neck had no strength to hold it up. "This isn't fair."

"What?"

"A voice that seduces, perfect coffee, and now a foot

massage." She groaned again. "Ohmigod, that feels good."

Jordan closed his eyes and applied himself to giving her the best damn foot rub she'd ever had in her life. "Relax," he ordered, though he was so rigid a mere touch would have shattered him.

She obeyed. She dropped flat to the glider and rested her head on her folded arms. Every few seconds she moaned in bliss, stretching her toes like a cat being petted.

Jordan was so hard he hurt. He desperately wanted to slide his hands up the backs of her firm thighs, to slip his fingers beneath the loose hem of the shorts she wore. Probably, he reasoned, she'd thought the shorts to be unappealing because they were old and gray and faded. But the material hugged her curves and they were loose enough in the legs that he could now see all the way to the tops of her thighs.

He slid his hands up her warm, resilient calves. She had excellent muscle tone, and even as he stroked her, kneading her flesh, feeling her muscles relax, he admitted he was beyond pathetic when a woman's muscle tone brought him to the edge.

Feeling like a damn lecher, he lifted one of her legs and was even able to see the edge of her panties, which—contrary to all he'd been telling himself—nearly made him erupt with carnal greed.

In a rasp totally unlike his normal seductive tone, he said, "Agree to my help, damn it."

She sighed, adjusted her head more comfortably and murmured in a barely there voice, "It wouldn't be right."

Affronted, Jordan realized she was on the verge of

sleep. Conflicting emotions bombarded him. Lust was there, tearing at his resolve, making his guts cramp, but there was also a throbbing explosion of tenderness, enough to expand his heart and tighten his lungs.

"I want to help you, Georgia."

She sighed, and in the next instant started to snore softly. A reluctant smile curved his mouth. Never in his benighted life had a woman fallen asleep on him. It was a novelty he could have lived without, but then it occurred to him that perhaps this was exactly what he needed to gain the upper hand.

"Georgia?" He continued working the tendons in her feet, something he knew from experience that all women seemed to enjoy. Personally, if a female was going to rub him, he could think of better places than his feet.

She didn't reply and after he gently placed her foot in his lap, he reached up and shook her shoulder.

She never stirred.

Jordan sat back with a grin. She'd said her children were very sound sleepers and now he knew that it was an inherited trait.

Beyond his feelings of triumph—because he really did have her now—it dawned on him that she was as vulnerable as a woman could be with a man, so she must trust him to some degree. And he wasn't above taking advantage of it.

He stroked her hair, silky soft and warm. He indulged his need to touch her, to learn the textures and curves of her face, her neck, her shoulder. Her spine was graceful, leading down to that superior rump that looked so damn tantalizing there before him, like an offering.

He was an honorable man, so he kept his hands on safe ground, but he looked at every inch of her, then whispered, "I've got you now, sweetheart."

And still she didn't move.

It took a lot of willpower to walk away from her, to find a blanket to cover her with and then to walk out of the room. But he managed it; he had a lot of fortitude when something really mattered.

And this mattered. Much as he hated to admit it, it mattered too damn much.

6

GEORGIA WOKE with the sunlight bright in her face. She didn't move, at first making an attempt to orient herself. Something wasn't right. She squinted; why was there so much light?

As her eyes adjusted, she saw the huge oak in her backyard through dirty windows, stately and still, not a single leaf stirring. There must be no wind, she thought, now that the dreadful rain had obviously ended.

And then it dawned on her that she wasn't in her own bed where she should be, or she certainly wouldn't be looking at the backyard. She was, as incredible as it seemed, in the enclosed patio curled up on the glider under a quilt.

She was still putting those thoughts together in the cobwebs of her mind when she heard a faint, muffled laugh. Lisa, then Adam. They sounded happy and for just a moment she thought everything was as it was supposed to be, as it had been the day before. Her mother, an early riser, was probably making coffee and the kids liked to hang next to her, waiting for cereal, chattering nonstop. Georgia always got up when she heard the kids, even though she was still exhausted and even though she knew her mother would complain and tell her to sleep more—and then she heard another deeper, more masculine laugh.

Jordan!

She jerked upright so fast the glider rolled, nearly spilling her onto the floor. Her heart racing, she remembered everything, her near arrest, her mother's illness—that orgasmic foot rub Jordan had been giving her late last night.

She twisted to face the kitchen behind her, and sure enough, that was Jordan's rough-velvet voice whispering, "Shhh. We don't want your mother to wake up yet. She had a long night."

Adam, sounding a bit blurry as if he hadn't been awake long himself, said, "Mommy always gets up with us, even when grandma grouches at her 'bout it."

Lisa bragged, "She won't hear anything, but she always hears us. Even when we're quiet. Grandma says that's a mommy's sixth sense."

"You've got an excellent mommy." Jordan said that with conviction, and Georgia wondered if he meant it. More likely he was merely trying to appease the kids. "But today we'll try to let her catch up on sleep."

Lisa asked, "Can I have the next pancake?"

Pancake?

"Absolutely. I can't believe you've eaten two already. Are you sure they're in your belly? You didn't hide one behind your ear?"

Lisa laughed again and Adam joined her.

Georgia nearly choked. She'd been sleeping so soundly one minute, and jarred awake the next, that she felt nearly drunk as she staggered to her feet in righteous indignation and groped her way toward the kitchen. Jordan was feeding her children? He had invaded her kitchen? What in the world was he doing here so early? The kids knew better than to go anywhere near the doors without her or their grandmother. She'd reminded them again and again that they were never ever to open the door to anyone.

Georgia stopped in the entryway, her thoughts scattering at the sight of Jordan. He looked...*gorgeous*. Sinfully gorgeous. His light brown hair was mussed, his jaw rough with beard stubble, his sleeves rolled back over his thick forearms. And he wore an apron around his waist.

For the first time she understood the appeal of "barefoot and pregnant in the kitchen". Jordan's bare feet looked very sexy, and though he wasn't in the family way, he was being domestic—which she assumed was the point. He smiled at Lisa and it made her heart expand painfully against her rib cage. Georgia rubbed a hand under her breast, trying to ease the constriction, but it didn't help.

God, the man looked good standing at her stove. He looked good with her children, too. And he looked far, far too good in her life.

Both kids wore aprons as well, tied up under their armpits and with the hems dragging near the floor. They were huddled around the stove while Jordan used a turkey baster to put pancake batter on the griddle with complex precision.

"I'm an artist," he proclaimed, and both kids quickly agreed.

Curiosity swamped her, and when she finally got her hungry gaze off Jordan and onto the griddle she saw that he was making the most odd-shaped pancakes she'd ever seen. They were...well, they looked like faces. And fish. And...

"Mommy!"

Adam rushed to her, nearly knocking her off her feet as he barreled into her legs. Jordan looked up with a frown. Lisa ran to her and took her hand.

It was traditional for them to share kisses and hugs first thing in the morning, and this morning was no different.

It wasn't traditional, however, for a very large, very sexy man to be looking on. A man with noticeable chest hair showing through the open collar of his shirt. A man with very warm, appreciative eyes.

Maybe the kids hadn't let him in. Maybe—she gulped—he'd spent the night! She couldn't seem to remember anything after he'd started working on her feet. Nothing except how incredibly good it had felt.

Heat rushed into her face and Jordan smiled as if he knew exactly why she blushed. Georgia ignored him, holding both children close, relishing the feel of their small arms tight around her neck, their sweet, familiar smells. She could never truly regret the mistakes in her life, because it was those mistakes that had given her Lisa and Adam.

But that didn't mean she wanted to make those mistakes again. Having a male stranger invade her life so easily not only showed her irresponsibility, but her stupidity. She couldn't let it happen. She *wouldn't* let it happen.

She'd barely straightened when both kids began extolling Jordan's virtues, how funny he was, his culinary expertise, his artistic talent. He'd already promised to show them new kittens at his office, and to take them along the next time he had to treat a horse or cow.

Like a damn new puppy, they wanted to keep him. Forever.

Georgia ground her teeth together and concentrated on getting her sluggish brain in gear. Adam demanded her attention with the typical enthusiasm of a four-year-old boy.

It was an effort, but Georgia hefted his sturdy little body into her arms. He clasped her face and said, "We been cookin'!"

"So I see." Her words ended on a jaw-splitting yawn and since her hands were full holding up her tank of a son, she couldn't quite cover her mouth.

Jordan ushered Lisa away from the stove with a gentle touch. "Not too close, hon. I want to get your mother some coffee before she topples over, and you never know when a pancake might explode. So don't go near the griddle without me, okay?"

Lisa held her sides as she laughed, but she did as he asked, settling into her chair at the table.

Without her permission, Jordan relieved her of Adam's weight, holding her son as if he had the right, as if he'd known how unsteady she still felt, and to her further annoyance, Adam clung to him.

Cooking, coffee, foot massage, and now coddling her kids; the man knew his way into a woman's heart.

Jordan handed her the coffee cup as a replacement for Adam. "Here. You look like you could use this."

Fragrant steam rose from the cup, making the coffee impossible to resist. She took one long hot sip and felt her head begin to clear. "Nothing on earth," she said with relish, "tastes better than that first sip of coffee in the morning."

His eyes took on a warm glow. "Oh, I don't know about that." He looked at her mouth, and heat shot down her spine, doing more than the coffee had to revive her.

Jordan smiled at her as he deftly seated Adam at the table and put a square pancake on his plate. "Why don't you sit down, Georgia, and I'll tell you what the hospital had to say this morning."

Her brain threatened to burst. Georgia glanced at the clock and saw it was only eight. "You've called them already?"

"Yes. I thought you'd probably want to know something as soon as you woke."

He was right, of course. Not only did he excite her, he read her mind.

"They said your mother rested peacefully through the night and that she's doing much better this morning. The doctor will be in to see her sometime between eleven and one, so I thought you'd like to be there." He looked her over, taking in the rumpled clothes she'd slept in. "I'd planned to wake you in an hour or so to give you time to get ready."

Wake her? She was both relieved and slightly disappointed to have missed that happening. She couldn't remember the last time she'd been awakened by a man. Before the divorce, she was always the one up first. To have Jordan wake her...it would have been a novel experience.

Dazed, Georgia looked around the kitchen. For the first time she could remember since moving in, it was spotless. Not a dish out of place, other than the ones now loaded with the odd pancake shapes. The counters were all spotless, the floor clean, the sink polished. Even the toys that were forever under foot had all been put away. The dozens of colored pictures by Adam and Lisa were neatly organized on the front of the refrigerator.

She frowned and cast a suspicious glare at Jordan. Had he been cleaning all night to accomplish so much? And why would he do such a thing anyway? Her father and her ex-husband had considered that women's work.

"Would you like a pancake?"

Her eyes narrowed at his continued good humor and solicitousness. "No."

"I can make it in the conventional shape if the fun stuff scares you."

He knew damn good and well that it was he who scared her, not his ridiculous pancakes. She considered strangling him.

"They're the best pancakes I've ever tasted!" Lisa said with her mouth full, her lips sticky with syrup. Georgia saw the box of pancake mix—the same that they always used—sitting on the cabinet, and raised her brows at Jordan.

"It's all in the preparation," he explained. "Any chef can tell you that."

She drank the rest of her coffee, in desperate need of the caffeine if she was expected to spar with him after just rising. Last night had been the best sleep she'd had in ages, when she'd thought she'd be awake fretting all night.

With that superior gentleness that made her want to smack him, Jordan took her arm and led her to a chair.

"Yes, there's more coffee," he said, saving her from having to ask.

He refilled her cup and she scowled. "Cooking, cleaning, serving. What are you? My fairy godmother?"

Leaning close to her ear, he whispered, "I'm just a man who wants you, sweetheart. And we did make that wonderful agreement last night."

She straightened so abruptly she bumped his chin with the back of her head. To his credit, he didn't curse, but he did give her a long look as he rubbed away the ache. Luckily the kids were digging into their food and not paying attention.

"What agreement?" she growled as he moved away, a man without a care in the world.

"We can go over all the details, as per your request," he said easily, "right after you get cleaned up and dressed."

"I don't remember any request!"

"Oh. Well, you were very groggy. Which was why you said it'd be better to finalize our plans—you do remember the plans?—in the morning." He turned to the stove and put three round pancakes on a plate, buttered them, and set them before her.

She had no recollection of the conversation at all. Certainly not about any plans. But those pancakes...the smells were incredible, making her stomach rumble loudly. Everyone looked at her. Lisa pointed and laughed.

Jordan pulled his own chair up close to hers. "When did you eat last?"

His gaze was too perceptive, too intrusive, demanding an honest reply. The problem was, she couldn't remember. The days tended to blur together when she worked double shifts.

He shook his head. "If you're going to burn the candle at both ends, you really need to refuel, you know."

"That's mixing your metaphors just a bit, isn't it?"

"Maybe. But the point is still valid, I swear." He watched her as she took her first bite, and smiled when she closed her eyes in bliss. "Good?"

"Very." She gave him a reluctant look, and added, "Thank you."

He touched her, stroking one long finger over her cheekbone and jaw, the side of her throat. "That wasn't so painful, now was it?"

Georgia froze for a heartbeat, mesmerized by that seductive tone and achingly tender touch. Then she shook herself and looked pointedly at her children, who were watching the byplay with an absorbed fascination. She supposed having a man at the breakfast table was even more unique for them. She doubted they remembered their father much, and what they would have remembered had nothing to do with peaceful family breakfasts together.

Jordan never missed a beat. "If you little beggars are done, why don't you go get your teeth brushed and pull on some clothes while your mother and I talk?"

"Talk about what?" Lisa wanted to know.

"Why, about you both visiting Casey again today, this time at our home. I live right near a long skinny lake. Casey can take you fishing while your mother and I visit the hospital and fetch your car back home from where she works."

Lisa and Adam immediately started jumping up and down, squealing and begging.

"That's enough," Georgia said. The kids quieted just a bit, but their eyes were still bright and wide with hope.

She stared at Jordan, her face so frozen it hurt, and murmured, "That's low, even for you."

He looked guilty for a flash of an instant, then resolve darkened his eyes. "I'm a desperate man. And we did make that bargain—"

"Kids," she interrupted, "go ahead and get dressed. And Lisa, remember you wanted to brush your teeth twice, okay?"

"Are we going to see Casey?"

Not if she could help it. "I'll have to think about it, sweetie. There's a lot I have to get done today."

The kids trailed out, dragging their feet, their expressions despondent. Damn Jordan for putting her in this position. Her children had so few outings these days, what with her working all the time. She knew how much they'd love a visit to a lake. But the more time she spent with Jordan, the weaker her stand on independence seemed to feel. She had to make it on her own. She *had* to.

When Georgia heard their footsteps at the top of the creaky stairs, she rounded on Jordan, blasting him with all her fury. "How dare you!"

After one long, silent look, Jordan began carrying dishes to the sink. "You're just being stubborn, Georgia. Why should the kids be cooped up at the hospital while you're visiting your mother? They'll enjoy being in the fresh air, and I already spoke with Casey this morning and he agreed—"

"*I didn't agree.*" She left her chair and faced him with

her hands on her hips. "They're *my* children and I know what's best for them."

"True." Jordan leaned back on the sink and silently studied her. "I'm not questioning your parenting skills, honey. It only took me about two seconds of seeing you with them to know how much you love them, and that they're crazy about you. But you did agree." When she stared at him blankly, he added, "Last night? Don't tell me you don't remember any of it?"

Her heart lurched at his continued insistence. Last night? So much of it, once he'd touched her feet, was a blur. She'd been so tired, so stressed....

"You told me," Jordan said calmly, "that taking the kids to Casey would be fine. Sawyer is going to meet me at the hospital, and while you're visiting, he and I will fetch your car. Afterwards we'll pick up the kids and I'll take you all to dinner."

Georgia felt like a deflated balloon. Surely she hadn't discussed all that with him? But he looked so positive, so sure of himself. And she *had* been beyond weary, ready to simply cave in under the exhaustion and worry. It was conceivable that she might have said things she now couldn't remember.

She just didn't know.

Her head hurt and she rubbed her fingers through her badly tangled hair. She felt Jordan's large firm hands settle on her shoulders and pull her close. She tried to resist him and the comfort, the security that he offered. She really did. But he brought her up flush against his strong, solid body and began rubbing her back. The man's voice wasn't the only thing magical about him. His fingers were pretty amazing, too.

It had been so, so long since anyone stronger, bigger than she had held her. Her muscles turned liquid at the wondrous feel of it.

Jordan's whiskery jaw brushed her temple as he spoke. "Just stop being so defensive and think about this logically, okay? We're not bad people, sweetheart. Casey will enjoy keeping your rugrats entertained for a few hours. He adores children. We all do. And Lisa already adores Casey. He's responsible. He won't let anything happen to them."

"But—"

He tipped up her chin. "But you're still worried? Please don't be. Not now. When things get straightened out and your mother is back home, then you can give me hell, okay?"

She couldn't help but laugh. "I don't want to give you hell. It's just that...I don't understand you."

"And that worries you?"

With complete honesty, she said, "Yes."

"Well, I don't quite understand myself right now, either, so I'm afraid I can't offer any explanations. I just know I want to help out. Is that so bad?"

She searched his face, looking for answers while confusion swamped her. "We barely know each other, Jordan."

"But it doesn't seem to matter, does it?" His gaze warmed and his touch changed. Just like that, he went from comforting to being all male. All interested male. He looked at her mouth and then kept on looking. "I can't believe how you make me feel."

"Jordan?" Her lips trembled. Her entire body trembled. Nothing should feel like this, so good and so scary and so...right.

He bent toward her. His breath teased her lips as he whispered, "What you do to me should be illegal."

Oh, the way he said that! He'd turned the full power of his bewitching voice on her and, combined with the memory of that sensuous foot rub of the night before, she was a goner. "Oh, my..."

He stole her breathy exclamation with his mouth as he kissed her. Knowing that she should resist, and being able to resist, were two entirely different things. His mouth was hot, incredibly hungry, and damp. She kissed him back, unable not to. His taste was indescribable. Hot and feverish. His hands were gentle on her face, a stark contrast to the consuming carnality of the kiss, eating at her, nipping with his teeth, sucking at her tongue as he groaned low in his throat and kissed her again and again.

Her hands curved around his shoulders and the feel of him, of solid muscle, bone and sinew flexing against her palms made her insides curl with raw desire. He arched her into his body and gave her his own tongue, tasting her deeply, pressing the hard planes of his body into her softness. Her breasts throbbed and ached, their galloping heartbeats mingled, and between her thighs....

Somehow she found herself backed up to the cabinets. With no effort at all, Jordan lifted her and the second she was balanced on the edge of the counter, he stepped between her thighs. She could feel the long, hard ridge of his erection, throbbing against her. His hand curved up her side and then over her breast, and it was so wonderful she cried out.

Jordan cursed as he kissed his way to her throat, to the sensitive skin beneath her ear. "I want you."

She wanted him, too. She held on to him, unable to think beyond the need. He was between her legs, leaving her open and vulnerable and she liked it. She liked the way he moved against her, stroking her with a tantalizing touch that brought her so close to completion even though they were both completely dressed and for the most part standing. She'd never realized that such a thing was possible, but she felt her muscles tightening, felt the spiral of delicious heat curling in her belly and below.

His fingertips brushed over her aching nipple, then pinched lightly and she almost lost it, almost came right there in her kitchen with a man who was hardly more than a stranger, a man who had no compunction about taking over her life. And she simply didn't care.

The kids started to argue upstairs and Jordan lifted his mouth. He was panting hard, his body shaking. His high cheekbones were slashed with aroused color, his emerald eyes burning. Heat poured off him.

In guttural tones that turned her limbs to butter, he growled, "I'm so damn hard right now, one touch and I'd be in oblivion." He squeezed her tighter, pressed his erection hard against her. *"One touch, Georgia."*

It appeared he expected a reply to that. But she could barely think clearly enough to stay upright on the countertop, much less know what to say. She stared at his mouth, her own open in mute surprise at all she'd felt, at how incredible a kiss and a few simple touches could be. She'd been married nearly seven years, but she hadn't known, hadn't guessed....

He muttered a raw curse. "Don't look at me like that. You're killing me."

She sucked in air and tried to think.

"Say something, damn it."

Nodding, Georgia looked around her kitchen, at all he'd done, at all he still apparently expected to do. Not just to the house, but to her as well. She knew as soon as her thoughts cleared, she'd be mortified. She'd broken her own rules, she'd breached propriety. She'd shamed herself this time more than ever before.

She met his gaze and swallowed. "I'm supposed to work tonight. I...I can't go to dinner."

HE SHOULDN'T have been so angry, but his emotions had been in a whirlwind since the first moment he saw her, and he hadn't gotten a firm handle on them yet. How could he have done something so stupid as to practically take her in her own damn kitchen, with her kids upstairs? Not only was he disgusted with his own lack of restraint, but he was madder than hell at himself for upsetting her.

Once she'd really had a chance to settle down and get her wits together, she'd looked devastated. Jordan could tell she didn't blame him. No, Georgia blamed herself, and he couldn't stand it. He'd wanted to lighten her physical load, and instead, he had added to her emotional one. He could only imagine what she was thinking, but she wouldn't look at him, and that pretty much told it all.

What was between them was damn powerful, and neither of them were coming to grips with it very well. Rather than discussing it, though, she'd informed him she had to work. Again.

Jordan put up a good front for the kids, trying to shelter them from his black mood, a mood he was afraid was partially caused by jealousy. He'd never felt it before, so he couldn't be certain, but he did know that he hated it, hated the way his muscles refused to relax, the way his stomach knotted every time he pictured her on that stage. Hiding his rage wasn't easy, but he'd take a punch on the chin before deliberately upsetting her again, or making her children uncomfortable.

He must have been somewhat successful, because the kids were subdued, but far from silent. Georgia had explained to them about hospitals, so they were wide-eyed with respect for the sick people, and apparently oblivious to his turmoil.

Despite her near stomping, Georgia's soft-soled shoes made no sound as they walked the length of the long hospital corridor. He could feel her nervousness and he wanted to protect her. He wanted to devour her.

He didn't want her blaming herself for the uncontrollable chemistry between them. And he did not want her dancing on that goddamn stage again.

They rounded a corner, the silence between them a living thing, and then they both drew up short as they saw not only Sawyer standing there, but Gabe and Casey as well. Oh, hell. His entire family just had to turn out, didn't they? If Misty hadn't been sick, no doubt Morgan would have been here now, too.

They were likely enjoying his predicament. He'd always been different from them. More withdrawn. More self-contained. Though he never doubted their love, he often felt like an outsider; because of his father, there were things he'd never be able to share with them. Like the pride of their male parentage.

Knowing he'd gotten himself mired in an emotional

conflict probably had them all rubbing their hands with glee. They just loved it when he fell into the same traps that grabbed them. It happened far too often for Jordan's peace of mind.

Lisa, being a natural-born flirt, smiled widely at the sight of Casey and took off at a run to see him. Casey grinned and knelt down to catch her. Adam quickly followed suit, but he was a bit more cautious, keeping one eye on Sawyer and Gabe.

Georgia had come to a complete and utter halt. She just stood there frozen, apparently as appalled as he felt. Jordan could have told her it wouldn't do her any good.

Sawyer started forward with a wide smile and a warm glint in his dark eyes. "Georgia?"

She nodded, staring up at him. Jordan heard her swallow. "Yes?"

Sawyer, damn him, hugged her. He put his arms right around her, as if she were a member of the family or something, and cradled her to his chest with a great show of affection.

Jordan saw red and had to struggle not to huff like a bull. Luckily Sawyer released her right away.

"It's so nice to meet you," Sawyer said. "Casey has told me quite a bit about you."

Her eyes were still round, her expression awed. "You're Casey's father?"

"Yes." Sawyer glowed with pride whenever he spoke of Case. "I understand he'll be doing a spot of baby-sitting today. We're all looking forward to it. Especially my wife. Now that we have our own little one—six-month-old Shohn—and with Morgan's daughter Amber, Honey's finding she really adores children. She's never had much chance to be around older children, so this'll be a real treat for her."

Jordan knew what his brother was doing, making it sound like a damn favor to him if Georgia didn't hesitate to let him take the kids. He'd told Sawyer on the phone that she hadn't quite agreed yet. But now, well...Sawyer's performance should clinch it.

He glanced at Georgia to see how she was reacting to Sawyer's long-winded introduction. He wasn't really surprised to see that her mouth was still open as she stared up at him. There was an innate compassion to Sawyer that drew women; they felt safe with him.

Then Gabe sauntered forward and Jordan thought she might faint. He cursed low even as he clasped her arm to steady her. Everyone ignored him.

"Hi, there," Gabe said, flashing her with his most engaging grin, and Georgia couldn't even blink. When Gabe waited, still smiling, she managed to lift one hand and flit her fingers in a feeble wave of greeting.

Jordan heaved a disgusted sigh. "Why are you all here?"

Sawyer shrugged. "I came because you asked me to. Gabe tagged along so you wouldn't have to leave Georgia here alone. He'll drive your car and drop me off to get Georgia's car, then we'll both be back. Casey is going to go ahead and take the kids to meet Honey, since she's practically bouncing with excitement."

Sawyer spoke as if the plans had all been finalized, attempting, no doubt, to head Georgia off at the pass, so to speak.

But at the mention of her offspring, Georgia came out of her stupor. "This is ridiculous. You're all going to so much trouble—"

"Not at all." Gabe winked at her, rendering her mute again. He had that effect on all women, it seemed. Even his wife wasn't yet immune. He'd ask Elizabeth if she'd like mashed potatoes, and the woman would blush scarlet. It was uncanny.

"It's no problem at all," Gabe assured her. "And for the record, my wife is anxious to meet the kids, too. We don't have any of our own yet. Not that I'm above trying, you understand—"

Jordan stepped in front of him. "You know, Georgia, since Sawyer is here anyway, why don't we let him take a peek at your mother? He's a damn fine doctor. And that way, if she ever has any other problems, you can just give him a call. They'll already be acquainted."

Sawyer nodded. "I still make housecalls, if you can believe the convenience of that! But in Buckhorn, we're all real neighborly that way."

Jordan shook his head at the not-so-subtle suggestion that Georgia could be more neighborly herself.

She turned her back on them all, one hand to her head. "This is incredible." She appeared to be speaking to herself.

"Where did you move from?" Gabe asked.

Distracted, she waved a hand and said, "Milwaukee."

"Ah, that explains it. We do things differently here."

She turned back around, her eyes intent. "Are there any other brothers I haven't met yet?"

They said in unison, "No."

"Thank God for small favors." They all grinned at her, making her fall back a step before she caught herself. "All right, I want to see my mother. I won't really feel reassured until I have. She's on the third floor."

Casey spoke up. "I'll go on and head out. The squirts are anxious to see the lake. That okay?"

Georgia looked harried, but she nodded. "Yes, okay." She pulled her children close. "You guys be on especially good behavior for Casey, all right?"

"We will!"

"We're always good."

Georgia smiled. "I know. I'm a very lucky mother to have you two."

The kids smothered her with hugs—quickly because they were anxious to be off—and she kissed each of them. "Jordan and I will be there soon. And be careful around that water!"

Casey put his arm around her shoulders and gave her a squeeze. "They'll be fine. Don't worry. We have a rule that no kids are allowed even on the shore without a life preserver on. I won't let them get hurt. I promise."

As Casey took both kids by the hand and walked away, Georgia got that shell-shocked look about her again.

Jordan gently maneuvered her into the elevator and pushed the third-floor button. In the crowded confines of the elevator, she stood closer to him than she had all morning. He assumed his brothers intimidated her because she was so damn small by comparison. Her curly golden brown hair would barely brush any of the male chins surrounding her, her shoulders were only half as wide as theirs.

Her petite build really emphasized her full breasts, he noticed. And once he noticed, he couldn't stop noticing. She wore a tailored yellow blouse buttoned to her throat and tucked into a long, trim denim skirt. There was nothing sexy about the outfit, and in fact, it was quite understated. But it did nothing to mask her appeal. He doubted a burlap sack could have managed that feat.

Jordan was lost in erotic fantasies better left to the privacy of his bedroom than a crowded elevator, when he felt her hand slip into his. He wanted to shout with the pleasure of it. She was warming to him, accepting him, even if reluctantly.

Then he saw that Sawyer had noticed it, too, and was whistling softly. He even nudged Gabe, who lifted both brows.

Jordan scowled at them. He could read their thoughts as clearly as if they were stamped on their foreheads. They liked it that he was exhibiting some male possessiveness. They'd reacted in a similar way when he'd had his first fight, ages ago. A few neighborhood bullies had been picking on an old dog, and when they'd thrown a rock and the dog had yelped, Jordan lost his temper. He'd been a young kid, but not too young to hate injustice and cruelty.

No one had been more shocked than he when he'd kicked butt on the older boys, but his brothers revelled in his loss of control. Since then, it had only happened a handful of times, but each and every time his brothers damn near had a celebration. It was as if they'd always known he could be ferocious, and loved seeing it firsthand.

Jordan had been disgusted with his loss of control then, just as he was now. Not that he would have done anything differently, but...

Before he could get truly annoyed with his brothers for being so smug at his predicament, the elevator doors opened.

Walking quickly now, Georgia made a beeline for her mother's room. Once there, she turned back to them as if not quite sure what to do with them. She glanced at Sawyer and Gabe, then to Jordan. "I might be awhile."

Jordan nodded. "Take your time. I'm in no hurry."

"Me, either," Gabe said, making her frown.

"Gabe and I will be on our way shortly," Sawyer promised her, "but I am interested in checking on your mother myself, if you're not opposed to it. It's not that I doubt the good care she's getting here. But with emphysema, any number of small ailments can come up. If you're comfortable with the idea, why then, I'm a whole lot closer than the hospital."

Georgia looked so relieved by the repeated offer, Jordan wanted to kiss her. Anytime she was given genuine caring, she always seemed so surprised.

"Actually," she said, "that would be wonderful. I worry so much about her. She says she won't overdo, but then something like this happens. She's so determined not to complain, to continue mothering me even when I don't need it, even though I'm twenty-three..."

Jordan nearly choked when she gave her age. Twenty-three? That had to mean she'd gotten pregnant at sixteen. Good Lord, that was a lot to expect of someone who was little more than a child herself. Had she finished high school? Gotten any college at all?

He again thought of her stepping onto that stage, and tried to imagine how she personally felt about it.

She was so damn young, so driven by hard-nosed pride. Did she enjoy the work at all or was she taking the only job she could that would pay the bills?

"Most mothers are that way," Sawyer assured her while casting quick worried glances at Jordan. "My own is as stubborn as a goat and twice as ornery."

Gabe nodded to that. When Georgia looked at Jordan, appalled by what she took as an insult to their mother, he managed to laugh to cover the emotions she'd made him feel. "You'd have to meet Mom to understand, sweetheart. We love her dearly, but—"

"But she did manage to raise the lot of you." Georgia shook her head. "I suppose that takes great fortitude."

They all laughed. "Exactly."

"Let me check on Mom and talk to her privately for a moment, to make sure she doesn't object to you coming in. I'll be right back."

Georgia slipped silently into the room and the second she was gone, Jordan began to pace. He could feel Sawyer and Gabe watching him.

"Any reason why you look so tormented?" Sawyer asked.

Jordan glared at him. "She's only twenty-three!"

"You thought she looked older?"

"No, Gabe, it's not that. It's just...damn she's young to do what she's doing."

Gabe asked, "What is it she's doing?"

Sawyer, having been apprised by Morgan, as well as Howard and Jesse who'd gotten a firsthand show, said, "I think he's talking about the dancing."

"Ah." Gabe caught Jordan's eye and gave him a

wide, masculine smile. "You know, I was thinking of going to watch her act, myself. I haven't seen a live show in ages. Whadya think, Sawyer? You want to come, too?"

7

JORDAN TURNED so fast Gabe jumped in surprise. With his eyes blazing and his jaw locked, he growled, "Don't even think about it, little brother."

After biting his lips to keep from laughing, Gabe soothed, "All right. Don't get in a lather over it."

It took him a second, and then Jordan's eyes narrowed. He realized Gabe had just gotten him but good. And Jordan had made it disgustingly easy for him to do. Choking Gabe sounded better by the minute.

Georgia opened the door. She looked at Jordan's severe frown, then at Sawyer's exasperation and Gabe's innocent expression. Her own turned suspicious. "Am I interrupting anything?"

"Not at all." Sawyer stepped forward. "Am I allowed in?"

She didn't look convinced, but she let it go. "Yes. Mom said she'd like to meet you." Georgia glanced once more at Jordan, then turned away. She and Sawyer walked into her mother's room, Sawyer's hand at her waist.

Jordan was still looking at the closed door when Gabe murmured, "I see Morgan was right."

Jordan rounded on his younger brother again. He

felt dangerously close to losing his edge. "You wanna tell me exactly what the hell that means?"

"Ho!" Gabe backed up, pretending fear. And this time there was no way for him to hide his amusement. "Don't bite my face off over a simple observation. If you're still worried that I might go to the bar, I promise I was just yanking your chain. You can quit snarling at me now. Besides, Lizzy would have my head if I looked at another woman and you know it. She's got a mean jealous streak." Gabe sounded immensely pleased over that observation.

"If you don't stop pricking my temper," Jordan rumbled, "you won't have to worry about Elizabeth. *I'll* have your damn head."

Gabe laughed. "Honest to God, Jordan, I've never seen you in such a fury. It's kind of interesting."

"You're on thin ice, Gabe."

In his defense, Gabe said, "Hey, I'm justified. Don't think I've forgotten that you stole my wife from me!"

Georgia gasped behind them. When they both turned to her, she stammered, "Mom wanted a moment alone with Sawyer." She looked from one to the other of them. She appeared stricken, and embarrassed.

Gabe smiled as he explained. "My wife chose to work for Jordan in his clinic. Jordan knew that I wanted her with me, but he made up all these lame excuses and just swept her away."

"That," Jordan said, watching Georgia closely, "is only Gabe's side of the story. Elizabeth has a knack with animals, a special rapport. She's much better suited to being my assistant than she is playing receptionist for Gabe. That's all he was referring to."

Gabe shrugged. "Well, you did kiss her, too. Right in front of me."

He snorted over that. "A brotherly kiss and you damn well know it."

"Brotherly, huh? Well, in that case—" Gabe reached for Georgia, who quickly took two startled steps away from him. But he'd barely moved more than a foot before Jordan caught him by his collar and hauled him back.

"Not in this lifetime, Gabe." The statement was low and mean, and made Gabe chuckle.

"That's what I figured." To Georgia, he said, "Can you believe he kissed my Lizzy? Not that I blame him. She's about the most beautiful woman in these parts and pretty irresistible. You'll see what I mean when you meet her. And luckily for Jordan here, I let him live because she turned right around after kissing him and agreed to marry me."

Georgia gave a nervous smile. "I see."

"No you don't." Jordan released Gabe and propped his hands on his hips. "Elizabeth had just helped me save all the animals in the clinic from a fire. It was a kiss of gratitude, no more."

"Uh-huh." Gabe pretended to think otherwise. "And what Morgan told me is that your Georgia here has incredibly pretty gray eyes. Now that I've seen her for myself, I agree. Very pretty."

He and Georgia spoke at the same time.

"She's not *my* Georgia."

"I'm not *his* Georgia."

Gabe said, "Oh, look. There's Sawyer."

They both turned and Sawyer nodded with a smile. "She's doing fine. Incredibly well, in fact. Her doctor is a good man. I've always liked him." Sawyer pulled out a card and handed it to Georgia. "Here's my home number. Once she's released, probably by the middle of the week, feel free to give me a call if you have any questions or if she has any problems, okay?"

Georgia's eyes softened to pewter. "Thank you. That's very generous of you."

"You might want to share that number with the children, too, so that if anything like this happens again, they can give me a call if you're at work."

She nodded as she tucked the card securely into her bag. "They have my number at the bar, but Bill doesn't always answer the phone at night during the show. We've argued over that several times."

"I understand." Sawyer glanced at Jordan. "Perhaps a pager would be good?"

Jordan saw the guilt flash across Georgia's face and knew she couldn't afford one. He spoke quickly. "Gabe, don't you have an extra pager you're not using anymore?"

Gabe looked dumbfounded for only a second, then nodded. "Oh, yeah. Right." And with a grin: "Hey, it's even paid up for the next six months."

Georgia was already shaking her head, but Gabe slung an arm around her, which caused her to still immediately. "I insist. That's what friends are for."

She might have protested further, once she regained use of her tongue, but Sawyer chose that auspicious moment to tell Jordan, "Her mother wants to see you."

"*Me?*"

"Yep. She was rather insistent on it."

Georgia groaned. "Oh, God. She's so overprotective...."

Jordan peered at the closed door with deep reservation. He hoped like hell this wasn't the familial interrogation. At thirty-three, he was so rusty he had no idea if he'd know how to answer or not. Especially considering he hadn't yet figured out what he felt for Georgia. Lust certainly, and compassion. But if there was more...

Georgia started to follow him in, but Sawyer gently caught her arm. "She specified that she wanted to see Jordan, and only Jordan."

Jordan groaned in dread, mustered his manly courage and headed in. He wasn't a damn coward. He could face one disgruntled mother, with or without all his thoughts in order. But when he peeked around the curtain to the bed, he found Ruth Samson half-sitting up, very clear-headed, and more than a little disgruntled.

Good heavens, the woman looked as ferocious as Morgan on his most intimidating days.

"MS. SAMSON?"

Her eyes, the same blue gray as her daughter's, locked onto him and without preamble she stated, "My daughter has whisker burns this morning."

Jordan gulped, and before he could stop himself he ran a hand over his now smooth-shaven jaw. Deciding to brazen it out, he said, "I only kissed her."

"Must have been one heck of a kiss." Ruth looked nothing like the frail, ill woman of yesterday. In truth, she appeared ready to get out of bed and whup Jordan's backside. "Georgia couldn't quite look at me without blushing."

Against his better judgment, Jordan grinned. "Georgia does seem prone to a pretty blush now and then."

Ruth sighed, and all the vinegar seemed to leave her from one second to the next. "It's incredible, but regardless of all she's been through, she's still so sweet. Not that I want her to toughen up. She's a wonderful daughter and a wonderful mother to my grandchildren." Once she said it, Ruth glared, daring him to disagree.

Jordan nodded. "She amazes me, if you want the truth."

"Yes. She's amazing." Her eyes sharpened and she asked, "Exactly how much do you know about my daughter?"

"Very little. I only just minutes ago found out she's a mere twenty-three."

"That bothers you? Well it shouldn't. Georgia is very mature for her years."

Jordan had no idea how to reply to that. "I also know that she works in a pretty disreputable bar."

Ruth laughed. "And of course, you don't approve?"

Jordan matched her stare without hesitation. "No, not at all."

"Good." She nodded in satisfaction. "Neither do I. But she has few choices."

"Georgia mentioned that to me."

Ruth looked surprised. "She did? That's interesting. She usually won't give a man the time of day. And believe me, plenty of them are after her."

Jordan ground his teeth together. "I believe it."

"I can tell there's still a lot you don't know. Pull up a chair and I'll fill you in. But we better be quick because if I know my daughter, we maybe have about two minutes more before she barges back in."

Jordan obediently pulled up a chair. He was anxious to learn more about Georgia, to find out how she'd ended up in these circumstances. She and her mother both felt she had few options, but Jordan intended to give her several, and they all had to do with her staying off that damn stage.

Ruth's first burst of indignant anger had faded and had left her looking decidedly limp. She was now pale, her hands shaking. Jordan reminded himself that the woman had been extremely ill only the night before, and that he had to make certain she didn't overdo. He had the feeling she'd push herself, given half a chance, to defend her daughter. *Against him.*

"Ms. Samson," he said, hoping to reassure her, "you don't have to worry about me being with Georgia. I only want to help."

She sighed wearily, then started in coughing. Jordan was ready to call for a nurse when she waved him back into his seat.

She had to use her oxygen for a moment, taking slow shallow breaths, and afterward she took quite a bit of time resetting her blankets around her. Finally she said, "I seriously doubt Georgia wants your help."

"Well, no, she doesn't."

"But you're insisting?"

"Yes, ma'am."

She nodded, apparently pleased by that. "Georgia got pregnant when she was only sixteen."

Since he'd already done the math, Jordan didn't show a single sign of surprise.

"My husband was an old-fashioned man. A sour, undemonstrative man who never really understood Georgia. We had her late in life. I was nearly forty, and my husband was eleven years my senior. We'd thought we were past the stage of having children. So she took us both by surprise."

"A pleasant surprise?"

"Oh, surely. But adjusting wasn't easy. Avery was set in his ways, and part of those ways was being miserly to the point of wanting Georgia to wear second-hand clothes, and insisting we drive our old Buick forever, and that we make do with one old black-and-white television. It had never mattered much to me. But I hated seeing Georgia do without. She didn't fit in with the other kids because of how we lived, and it wasn't even necessary. We could have afforded better for her, but I'd always been a housewife, and Avery had always controlled the money."

Jordan nodded. "I understand." And he did. He knew plenty of older women like Ruth, women who'd been raised to believe that wives were meant to stay at home, to cater to their husbands. He could only imagine how a child thrown into the mix might have complicated things.

"Well, I don't. I could have done more. And I could have done it sooner." Ruth looked past Jordan's shoulder, her eyes so sad. "We argued endlessly over Georgia, which was probably harder for her than the divorce. I was a coward, and the idea of being on my own was terrifying. But I finally did it. I should have left him years earlier, but I kept thinking that I needed to keep our home intact. I didn't want Georgia to have to start over in a new school system just because I couldn't afford the area anymore. Then, when she started dating Dennis Peach I wished like crazy that I *had* moved."

"She got pregnant?"

"Yes. Dennis was every young girl's dream. He was good-looking, athletic, nice. He took her to all the dances and the parties, places she hadn't been before. Georgia went head over heels in love with him almost overnight.

"We were still hashing out the divorce when Georgia eloped. I couldn't believe it. But to give her her due, she made things work for awhile there."

Jordan imagined that Georgia had enough sheer will and determination to make anything work when she put her mind to it. He thought about her at that age, so young, so innocent. At sixteen, he'd been into more mischief than his mother ever guessed, but he'd been careful, with himself and the girls he'd been with.

He resolved to have another talk with Casey real soon. It wouldn't hurt to drive the point home one more time.

"Dennis wasn't too bad," Ruth said. "They lived like paupers, but then Georgia was used to that. And she seemed so happy, especially after Lisa was born. My gosh, she adored that baby. She took to mothering as natural as could be."

Jordan didn't want to hear about how happy she'd been with her husband. He was glad the man was long gone from the picture. "So what happened?"

"Her in-laws happened. They made life as tough for

Georgia as they could. While she was willing to make sacrifices for the marriage, Dennis wasn't used to living without. They coddled him something awful, and ignored Lisa—even to the point of questioning whether or not she was his. I tried to help out as much as I could, but I was dealing with the issue of my divorce and somehow Georgia ended up helping me."

Ruth looked so wretched over that admission, Jordan reached out patted her hand. "Your daughter loves you very much."

"I know." She spoke barely above a whisper. "My husband had always smoked and right after the divorce I started getting sick. I tried to find a job, but I had no experience and I'd get winded so easy. More so than most people, I'm prone to getting bronchitis and even pneumonia. That's when they found out how bad my lungs are. Only by then, I didn't have any health insurance because I'd been covered under my husband's policy. I was so, so stupid not to think of that."

Jordan wondered if Georgia was paying for insurance for her mother. He frowned with the thought, mentally adding up all her responsibilities.

"I was a burden to my daughter at a time when she needed me most."

"No." Jordan shook his head, knowing exactly what Georgia would have to say about that. "That's not true. Family helps family. Period. She was there for you, just as you're here for her now. She's told me several times how much you contribute."

Ruth tilted her head. "You sound like a man with a close family."

"Yes. Like you, my mother is divorced." His

mother, however, had always been one of the strongest, most independent women he knew. Of course, she'd had a fabulous first husband who'd shown her exactly what marriage should be. And that had thankfully gotten her through her marriage to Jordan's father.

Jordan forced a smile for Ruth's benefit. "She's also happily remarried. Through it all, we've stayed a very close family."

"I like you, Jordan."

She said that as if he'd passed a test. "I like you, too."

"And you like my daughter?"

When he hesitated, not quite sure how she meant it and afraid of committing himself to her, she laughed. "That's all right. I didn't mean to pressure you. But I will tell you that it's not going to be easy."

"I already figured that out."

She laughed again. "The end of this long tale is that shortly after Georgia got pregnant with Adam—an accident, and a blessing from God—Dennis's parents convinced him that he was overburdened, that Georgia had gotten pregnant on purpose just to chain him down." Under her breath she muttered, "As if a broken condom was her fault."

That was *definitely* not an image Jordan wanted haunting his brain. He frowned.

"Dennis had always been pampered, and as their bills started to pile up and things got tougher and tougher, he got more and more distant, more willing to run home to his parents. And unfortunately, more willing to run up additional bills. Their combined incomes just weren't enough, and one day he went home to his folks and never came back."

Jordan nodded in satisfaction. "So she divorced him?"

"Yes. Georgia was really hurt. She loved him and yet he just walked away. She agreed to a peaceful divorce, and allowed the courts to divide the bills down the middle even though many of them had been his recent purchases. She wanted to make the transition as easy on the children as she could. But the really sad part is that Dennis agreed to it all, wished Georgia well, then stole several thousand dollars from his parents and took off. Not only did he not pay his half of the bills, he's never paid a dime of child support."

"He doesn't see the kids?"

"No. No one's heard from him since he left. His parents blamed Georgia, and added to her burden—until I told them I'd have the police after their precious son for skipping out on his responsibilities."

She looked downright feral again, and Jordan nodded. "Good for you."

"No, it was an error in judgment. His parents apologized and promised to pay Dennis's share of things. Georgia argued with them. They were Dennis's bills, not his parents. But they insisted, and she believed them. She...trusted them. In the end, they were only biding their time until they could petition the court for custody of Adam and Lisa. They even tried to accuse Georgia of being an unfit mother."

Rage churned forth in Jordan, taking him by surprise. In a voice of icy rage, he said, "They obviously failed in their efforts."

"Yes. But not without a lot of cost and heartache to

my daughter. And they didn't give up. They dogged her steps everywhere she went, making her lose jobs, constantly posing a threat to her peace of mind. Not once have they ever shown genuine concern or caring for the children. The few times they visited them, they tried to fill their heads with poison, bad-mouthing Georgia while making Dennis sound like a saint that she'd run off. Can you imagine? Their own blood kin, yet all they're interested in is using the kids to try to hurt Georgia."

"They're beautiful children," Jordan said with sincerity. He'd been surprised at how much he'd enjoyed making pancakes with them that morning. Lisa and Adam were lively and bright and polite. "She's done a good job with them."

"Yes, she has. And she'd die before letting anyone hurt those kids. So finally we thought it was best to simply move away. It makes me so mad, I want to spit."

Jordan could easily see where Georgia got her backbone. He patted Ruth's hand and tried to calm her. "Don't get yourself all riled up. You'll get winded again and the doctors will throw me out." He smiled. "Besides, Georgia is here now, away from them, and the kids seem very happy. I wish she hadn't gone through so much, but all in all, I admit I'm pleased with the outcome."

"Moving here was a blessing," Ruth agreed. "And you know, it was my ex-husband who made it possible."

Jordan raised a brow. He hoped the man had somehow redeemed himself, had supported his daughter

and her decisions—mistakes included—after all.
"How's that?"

"He died."

Not the happy ending he'd been looking for. Jordan
sighed, wishing Georgia had been able to resolve
things with her father before his death, but he had the
feeling even that had been denied her.

"He hadn't ever gotten around to changing his will.
He had money that he'd hidden during our divorce. It
all came to me. Not that there was a fortune or anything. But it was enough to finance the move and put
a down payment on the house. I just hate seeing Georgia work so hard to keep it all together."

"I intend to help her with that."

Ruth shook her head. "She won't like it. Everyone
she's ever relied on has let her down. Her father, her
husband, her in-laws. She's determined to be totally
independent this time."

"You never turned your back on her."

"No, but I made some awful mistakes."

Jordan pushed to his feet, anxious to see Georgia
again now that he had a better understanding of her.
"Making mistakes is the name of game. We're human,
so it happens. Trying to atone for mistakes is what
makes you a mother."

She grinned at that. "True. So what are you going to
do?"

"I don't know yet."

"One thing, Jordan, before you leave."

"Yes?" He turned to face her.

"If you think there's any chance at all you might
hurt her, it'd be better if you walked away right now."

Jordan stared down at his feet. He didn't want to

hurt her. Ever. But even more than that, he didn't want to walk away. He wanted to gather her closer, much closer. He wanted to bind her to him in some undeniable way.

He made plans for the coming weeks, how he'd ingratiate not only himself, but his best selling tool—his family. They were irresistible, and once Georgia got comfortable sharing with them, relying on them and letting them rely on her, she'd soften. She had to.

Jordan shook his head. No doubt about it, he was in over his head. But damned if he wasn't starting to like it.

8

WITH AN OUTRAGED and appalled gasp, Georgia slapped the stage curtain back into place. "Damn him!" Her heart felt lodged in her throat, and with a lot of trepidation, she looked down at her costume.

"Oh, God." It looked worse than she'd first thought, given that Jordan was about to see her in it. Again she pulled the curtain aside and peeked out. But Jordan was still there, sitting at a front-row table as had become his preference, scowling at every other man in the room. He resembled a dog guarding a bone.

What in the world was wrong with him? She should have been able to ignore him, and in fact, when he'd first shown up as part of the audience, she hadn't even realized he was there until she'd almost finished. She made it a point not to look at the men in the audience; it was the only way she could get through putting herself on display that way. But she'd felt something different that night, something that had affected her deep inside. Against her will her gaze had sought out the source of her discomfort—and clashed with Jordan's hot green stare.

She'd missed a step and nearly fallen on her face. He'd looked as menacing as Morgan ever had. Of course, now that she knew Morgan better, she knew most of his dark countenance was bluster. Not so with

Jordan. His brothers insisted on telling her—in private little whispers—that Jordan was the most even tempered one, the pacifist, the gentlest of men. Ha! Twice now, he'd almost started another fight.

Bill had threatened to ban him from the bar and Georgia had silently prayed that he'd follow through. But then Jordan had slipped her boss a twenty, and Bill had grinned and walked away. Curse him.

The music was getting louder, her cue had come and gone, and she could hear the rumble of impatient voices out front. If she didn't get going, she'd have to start the CD over.

She lifted her chin. So what if this particular costume left her stomach bare? That you could see her navel? So what that more of her backside showed than was covered? All that meant was that her tips tonight would be especially good and she'd finally be able to afford the electrical work needed on the house. If Jordan didn't like what she wore...well, too bad. She wasn't too crazy about him right now anyway.

Determination masking her churning nervousness, Georgia thrust the curtain aside and made an entrance onto the stage. She had every intention of ignoring Jordan completely.

Of course, that was before he fell off his chair.

He took one look at her, dropped his cola and toppled. Luckily no one seemed to pay him any mind as he hauled himself back up and into his seat.

Georgia deliberately turned her back on him—and heard a roar of applause along with some loud wolf whistles, likely because the bottom of her costume was no more than a thong. Embarrassment washed over her, so hot she felt light-headed and couldn't see beyond the fog of shame. She knew she was blushing. *Everywhere*. The dance steps that normally came so easily to her now felt forced and awkward; she had to concentrate hard to keep to her rhythm.

At least, she told herself as she executed a high kick, her top was more concealing. It had midlength sleeves and a V-shaped neck with lapels. The whole outfit was stark white, including the stupid little hat that Bill had insisted on. She wore white gloves, white high-heel sandals, and garters with black velvet ribbons.

It looked cheesy, like something out of a fetish catalogue. But already money landed at the front of the stage. Georgia moved farther back, being careful not to lose her footing on the scattering of bills.

By the time she finished her number, she figured there had to be a good three hundred dollars at her feet. Not bad for a night's pay. She almost smiled. *Almost*.

And then she accidentally caught Jordan's eye.

He looked livid, with his eyes sort of red and unfocused. Georgia frowned at him. How such a dominating, stubborn, pushy man could have such nice relatives was beyond her.

With one last bow, she turned and ducked behind the curtain. Her changing room was really a cleaning closet overflowing with supplies. Next to her street clothes hanging on a metal hook, rested a mildewy mop and several stained rags. One bare bench, raw enough to leave splinters in her behind if she was ever foolish enough to sit on it, occupied the space next to the door.

Georgia tossed the foolish hat aside, then leaned against the wall and struggled to catch her breath.

Dancing, even at the bar, always left her exuberant. She loved to dance, to feel her movements become fluid like the music. And thanks to Jordan, she no longer had to go on stage in a state of exhaustion. He and his family had forced so much help on her, had been so supportive and friendly and accepting, she'd gotten plenty of rest the past few weeks.

But while she was grateful, she was also resentful because it was Jordan's fault that she hesitated to answer tonight's screaming applause with an encore. She just couldn't make herself go back out there. Not with Jordan watching.

Bill pounded on her door. "Front and center, damn it! They're calling for you."

Georgia stared at the closed door. She could probably convince Bill that it was better to leave them wanting more....

Then Jordan's voice intruded. "If she doesn't want to go back out there, then leave her alone."

She gasped in outrage. How dare he confront her boss? Was he trying to get her fired?

She answered her own question with an obvious, resounding yes. Not once had Jordan tried to hide his disdain of The Swine. This time, however, he'd stepped completely over the line.

The door bounced hard against the wall when she threw it open. Both Jordan and Bill jumped, but Georgia stomped right past them to the steps leading up on stage. It was uncanny, but she could actually feel the searing heat of Jordan's gaze on her exposed rump.

The second she opened the curtain, the men bellowed their appreciation. More money came flying her way and Georgia, with grim resolve, submitted to the attention.

After three encores she was finally left in peace.

For all of one minute.

She'd just stepped out of her high-heel sandals and started to relax when Jordan walked in without knocking. His gaze did the quick once-over, searing her from head to toes and everywhere in-between. Georgia glared at him. "What are you doing here?"

Despite his heated expression, his tone sounded mild enough. "I was already out."

She didn't buy it for a second. "Try again, Jordan."

"All right." He didn't appear the least put off by her hostile attitude. But then, she'd already realized how pigheaded he could be in his determination. "I stopped by to see your mother. She had the kids in bed, so I missed visiting with them. We took tea in the patio room, and when she started yawning, I told she should turn in, too. Though she's doing so much better, Sawyer says she should continue to get plenty of rest."

His words were easy and rehearsed. But his gaze burned over her, lingering in places that always felt too sensitive whenever Jordan Sommerville was in the vicinity.

Realizing she still wore the stupid gloves, she jerked them off and stuffed them into her bag. Jordan leaned against the wall, crossed his arms over his chest, and watched her every movement with an intensity that set her stomach to roiling. She couldn't very well finish changing with him standing there.

"It's rude to stare," she grumbled.

"Honey, the whole point of that getup is to make men stare."

She lost it, stepping forward and poking him hard in the chest. "Not *you!* Other men, okay, men who want to watch me dance, men who—"

Rubbing at his chest and frowning at the same time, Jordan interjected, "I came to watch you dance."

"No, you came to watch everyone else watch me dance!" Her head pounded, keeping time with her heart. She felt ready to burst into tears, to scream. He and his family were so wonderful, so giving, they made her feel terrible in comparison. All her life she'd screwed up. Having Jordan around only emphasized that, and weakened her resolve to learn independence. But she needed to know she could protect her children now, and in the future.

"You," she said in a tone nearing a snarl, "came to make sure no one did anything improper like *speak* to me."

Jordan took his own step forward. "Are you telling me you *want* to converse with these yahoos?"

"I'm telling you it's none of your damn business what I do!"

Jordan stalled, then in a voice as soft as warm velvet, he whispered, "I want it to be my business, though. Keeping my hands off you the past few weeks has been torture. Hell, Georgia..."

Her heart slammed into her ribs. He reached for her, touched her face with a gentleness she'd never known, and her knees went weak. "Jordan?"

Even to her own ears, his name sounded like a plea. The past few weeks had been hell, with the memory of his touch haunting her. She'd dreamed about that morning in the kitchen, and every night the dreams got hotter, more real.

Jordan cupped her jaw. "Don't ask me to go away, sweetheart. And don't ask me not to care."

Georgia watched his eyes darken, now so close to her own since he loomed over her. She exhaled on a trembling sigh. "You're making me crazy," she admitted. "I don't even know what I'm thinking or saying anymore."

His gaze flickered, becoming more intimate, hotter. "I don't mean to upset you."

"I know that." She almost laughed, it was so absurd. Jordan and his family had irrevocably changed her life—all for the better. Casey cut her grass, Gabe fixed her leaky pipes, they all doted on the children and on her mother. And on her.

But what if she came to depend on them, if she let her children start to love them, and then they went away? What would she do then? She'd be no better off, and she'd have the memories to torment her.

She squeezed her eyes shut, but quickly opened them again when Jordan's big thumb teased at the corner of her mouth. "Jordan," she said, hoping to make him understand, "dancing on that stage is hard enough for me. Especially in this getup. I do what I have to do, but I don't like it. When you're here, passing judgment and waiting to condemn, well...it only makes me more nervous."

Jordan shook her gently. "I'm not condemning *you*. How could you even think that?"

"You condemn all this." She'd learned so much about him from his family. Her visits with them had started out strained, but Honey wasn't a woman who left anyone feeling uncomfortable, and his brothers were too outrageous to be kept at an emotional distance. They treated her with all the teasing irreverence normally reserved for a little sister. And she loved it.

Where Jordan tended to close up about anything personal, his brothers took delight in sharing his deepest darkest secrets. Gabe had told her that Jordan never drank. And Morgan had told her because of his father, he protested any abuse of alcohol.

Georgia shook her head. "You may not condemn me specifically, but the bar, the men here, the atmosphere... And I'm a part of it, Jordan." She hesitated, unsure how much she wanted to push him, especially in a damn closet, but she just couldn't take it anymore.

She stepped away from him and concentrated on what she had to say while putting away her high heels. "You've done so much for me. I never would have gotten through the past weeks without your help."

"Nonsense. You're about the most resourceful woman I've ever met. I have no doubt you'd have managed just fine. But you know I wanted to help."

His praise made her feel more vulnerable than ever. "And I appreciate it more than I can say. You're...well, you're wonderful."

Jordan stared at her hard. "But?"

She drew a deep breath, forcing herself to say the words. "But I want to make it on my own. It's important to me. I've made some really dumb mistakes in the past, mistakes that have hurt me, my children and my mother. I'm trying to fix all that."

"You can't fix the past, sweetheart. All you can do is make the future different."

She nodded. "I know. And that's what I'm going to do. My mother insists she's feeling as good as ever, and I've cut back on the hours I work during the day so she's not overburdened with the kids. And thanks to Bill's stupid costume choices, I'm making more money in the evenings so my budget is more sound than ever. I'm managing, Jordan, and that's what I want to concentrate on."

Jordan gave her a long, considering look. As if she hadn't just spilled her guts to him, he said, "Your mother likes me."

Georgia had no idea how to respond to that. Truth was, her mother adored him.

"Your kids are crazy about me."

She smiled. "I know. They're also crazy about your family. Honey has been promoted to honorary aunt. Morgan, that big ox, astounds me every time he manages to be so gentle with them. And Sawyer and Casey..." She shook her head. "They're incredible men."

Jordan stepped closer until his chest brushed her breasts. "We're your friends now. You can't just expect us all to go away."

"I wouldn't want that!" It was so difficult to think clearly with him this close. She wanted to wrap her arms around him, to ask him to hold her. But he hadn't touched her sexually since that morning in her kitchen, and she knew that was for the best.

"My children," she said slowly, measuring her words, "have never had enough people in their lives who cared about them. My ex-in-laws..." She shook her head, not willing to go into details. "They weren't nice people. They've never really cared about Lisa or Adam."

"They must be idiots, then, because your children are very lovable."

Anyone who loved her kids automatically got her love as well. And that fact scared her to death.

Feeling almost desperate, she put a hand on his arm and explained, "I want to keep the friendship." She wanted that so badly her stomach felt like lead whenever she thought of losing it. As a child, she'd craved friendship so badly, always watching from the sidelines as someone else got picked for tag, as other girls gathered in clusters to giggle, excluding her. As a teenager, she'd put everything into her dance, detaching herself from the hurt, telling herself that she didn't care. She'd gone from being almost totally isolated from friends, to being Dennis's wife, then to being on her own again.

Gaining friendship only to lose it once more would be unbearable. "I just...I just don't want you here at night, watching me. I don't want it to go beyond friendship."

Jordan cradled her face between his large hands. She felt helpless against the drugging pull of his nearness, the warmth of his body, his scent. Everything he'd ever made her feel came swamping back with his first gentle touch.

"I'll tell you what I think." His sensual tone made her heart race. "I think everything you've just said is bullshit."

She stared at him, appalled, wondering if he could really see through her so easily.

"I think," he growled as he pulled her into the hardness and heat of his body, "that you want me every bit as much as I want you. Friends? Hell yes, we'll be friends. And a whole lot more."

She wasn't at all surprised when he kissed her.

JORDAN WANTED to devour her. The need she created just by being close nearly made him crazy. It was a live thing, a teeth-gnashing hunger that he had no control over. He groaned, sucking her tongue into his mouth and stroking it with his own.

Georgia's arms slipped around his neck, her soft breasts nestling into his chest. Her costume top was skimpy and he slipped his hands beneath it to feel the warm skin of her back, then couldn't resist sliding his hands down to her sweetly curved ass. His body pulsed with need, his erection growing painfully. Her bottom was bare except for the thong and her cheeks were hot, soft. He traced the thin line of material with his fingertips as deeply as he could, and took her rough groan into his mouth.

She went on tiptoe against him, pushing into him. Her nipples were hard and he used his other hand to explore her breasts. He wanted her naked. He wanted to see her nipples, to taste them.

He kissed her neck as he brought both hands up to the lapels on her top and pulled them open. The low vee of the costume made it easy to expose her and the second her breasts were freed, pushed up by the material bunched tightly beneath them, Georgia gasped. Jordan didn't give her time to pull away. He dipped his head down and licked one dark rosy nipple.

Her fingers clenched in his hair. *"Jordan."*

"Shhh." Even with his blood roaring in his ears, Jordan cautioned himself to go slow, to tease her, to make her admit to the incredible passion between them. All the well-grounded reasons to give her more time, to avoid sexual interludes, were chased away by the sight of her.

Her nipples were large, tightly puckered. He licked again, then again, using the rough tip of his tongue to torment her. Tantalizing sounds of hunger escaped her. He caught her with his teeth and nipped gently, then not so gently. Georgia trembled. When she tried to pull him closer he sucked her deep into the heat of his mouth.

"Jordan..." she whispered on a vibrating moan.

"I know, sweetheart, I know."

He cupped her between her legs. She was so hot, and she pushed against his probing fingers, her thighs opening without his instruction. He could feel her swollen flesh, feel the dampness of her even through the material. The bottoms were tight but he insinuated his fingers beneath the right leg opening and found her wet and ready—for him. He straightened and held her tightly with his free arm.

Her hips moved with his fingers, seeking more of his touch. Jordan felt swollen and thick, achingly hard. The damn saloon could have blown up and he might not have noticed. He was only aware of the feel of her, her scent, now stronger with her excitement.

"Come on, sweetheart," he encouraged roughly, seeing that she was already climbing toward a climax. Her eyes were cloudy, unfocused, her lips parted as she panted for breath. His fingers moved more deeply, stroking, sliding insistently over her slick flesh then up to her swollen clitoris. Delicately now, he touched her, light, rhythmic touches.

Georgia groaned and squeezed her eyes closed. Jordan watched her face, saw her skin flush darkly, her lush mouth tremble. Her pulse raced in her throat, and her hands bit into his upper arms, caught between pulling him closer and pushing him away.

"Come for me, Georgia," he groaned, knowing he, too, was perilously close to the edge. "I want to see you come."

Her beautiful breasts heaved, her throat arched, and then she bit her bottom lip and groaned harsh and low and Jordan supported her, mesmerized as she jerked and shuddered and it went on and on. He felt so much a part of her that he knew nothing would ever be the same again.

Long seconds passed. Gently, he pulled his fingers from her. Her eyelashes fluttered and she looked at him, still slightly dazed. Her forehead and temples were dewy, her breathing still labored. Jordan met her gaze, held it as he lifted his fingers to his mouth and sucked them clean.

Georgia shuddered. She clung to him with a rough tenderness he'd never known before. She was pliant, accepting of his will.

He gave her a kiss of lingering need and apology. Holding her, seeing her like this, brought him back to reality. The very last thing she wanted or needed was to be taken quickly in a damn saloon closet. Not that he regretted giving her pleasure. How could he?

"We have to stop." Jordan couldn't quite believe the words came from his own mouth. Not when he wanted her so badly. But the past few weeks had been a carefully wrought campaign to win her over, and he wouldn't blow it now. If he made love to her here—

and he was about a nanosecond away from doing just that—her embarrassment would drive a new wedge between them.

He took a deep breath and said, "I can't take you here, sweetheart." He kissed her damp, open mouth in quick little pecks, hoping to soften his next words. "Let's go somewhere else."

The slumberous, sated look left her eyes. Her cheeks, warmly flushed only seconds before, went pale. He knew before she answered that she'd refuse.

Georgia pushed away from him and covered her face with both hands. In a tone more startling for the lack of emotion, she whispered, "I can't believe I just did that."

Alarmed, Jordan smoothed her hair away from her face with trembling hands. "I can't believe I stopped."

She looked up at him. "You must think I'm awful."

"No." She started to say something more, but he didn't let her. "Shh. It's okay." Even with her heavy stage makeup, she looked precious to him. "Actually, it was better than okay. Much much better."

"But you didn't—" She glanced down at his very visible erection.

"Believe me, I know." Jordan ran a hand through his hair and tamped down his sexual frustration. He met her wary, shame-filled gaze, knowing his own was hot, piercing. "The thing is," he said, his voice sounding like sandpaper, "making you come was a helluva fantasy. And I wasn't disappointed."

"It was wrong."

"No. Hell, no. Nothing wrong can feel that right and you know it." He shook her gently. "Don't ask me to apologize, Georgia. We've both been on the ragged edge since first meeting and it was only a matter of time before this—and more—was bound to happen."

She attempted to turn away. "Please, don't come here again. I can't trust myself around you."

She asked the impossible. The first time he'd sat there and watched her dance, he swore he'd never come back. It ate him up to see all those men drooling over her, to know what they were thinking, that she was the center of so many drunken, lurid fantasies.

But he'd discovered that staying away was even harder. He couldn't sleep for wanting her; she occupied his thoughts both day and night. The few times he managed to get her out of his mind, he found himself thinking about the kids instead, smiling, missing them. And Ruth, too. She was such a gutsy woman, altering a lifetime of social conformity to stand up for her daughter.

"I'm not just here because of you." The second the words left his mouth, Jordan felt hemmed in by his own deceptions. He came because of Georgia, but he did have another purpose.

He truly detested the place, the smells of sour alcohol, sweat and dirt, the foul language and the overall atmosphere of depression. He considered The Swine a major nuisance, perhaps even a threat to the peace. It wasn't a quaint small-town saloon. It didn't provide lively conversation or a relaxing ambiance.

It was run-down, dirty and bred trouble because of a distinct lack of conscience on the owner's part. It didn't matter how staggering drunk the patrons might be, they could always get one more drink.

But because of Jordan's personal bias against alcohol, he'd have left others to deal with the bar if it hadn't been for Georgia. With her working at night, dressed so provocatively, he couldn't bear the thought of any of his friends or acquaintances seeing her.

Georgia looked shaken to her soul. She turned away and began pulling on her clothes over the costume. "If...if you're not here because of me, then why?"

"I'm here," he said gently, trying to ignore the demanding throb of his body, and the pleasant buzz of satisfaction despite his still raging lust, "because the Town Advisory Board had another meeting."

She turned to him with open anxiety.

"After Zenny and Walt and the others told them what they'd seen that first night, they've been outraged about the whole thing."

"Zenny and Walt?"

Jordan nodded. "I told you I was here with other men that first night? Well, they're the elders of the town, fairly set in their ways, too. When the trouble started they didn't even wait around to see how it'd turn out. They took off and by that next morning everyone in Buckhorn knew what had happened."

Her mouth opened and she breathed deeply. She stared at the far wall. "They know about me dancing?"

He nodded. "That, and the fact the police were called. I'd say folks are suffering equal parts of morbid fascination and outrage."

Georgia closed her eyes on a grimace.

He wanted to protect her from the opinions of others, but she deserved to know what was going on. Given a choice, many of the townsfolk would prefer the bar be shut down. That'd put Georgia out of a job, and into one hell of a predicament. "Sawyer and I cautioned them not to get up in arms, but then last night Morgan arrested two men who were menacing a mule."

Georgia's eyes snapped open again. "Menacing a *mule?*"

"That's right. They drove straight into a pasture, knocking down fence posts and tearing up the ground. The mule is a gentle old relic, but those bastards drove around with their horn blaring and their bright lights on, chasing her and scaring her near to death."

His fists clenched. He couldn't abide cruelty of any kind, but especially cruelty against women, children—or animals. "They're lucky Morgan found them instead of me. I'd have been tempted to teach them a better lesson than a night in jail, three-month suspension of their licenses, and a large fine."

Georgia's gray eyes were soft and sympathetic. "I thought you were the least militant one in the family."

"They were chasing a poor mule, Georgia, and they destroyed a good deal of property. Of course I'm feeling militant."

She touched his chest, her small hand gently stroking. Since his lust was unappeased, she nearly sent him into oblivion. "They had been drinking here?"

"That's right." Jordan felt far too hot. He wanted her hand on his bare skin. And he wanted it a good deal south of his chest. Just the thought of her slender fingers curling around his hard swollen flesh made him quiver like a virgin. He hurt with wanting her. "Your boss," he rasped, "knew they were drunk when they left here."

She nodded. "Bill could care less as long he's getting paid.

Jordan struggled for breath. He flattened his own hand over hers, stilling her caressing movements. "Morgan is meeting with the sheriff here. He thinks they might hit the bar with a heavy fine." Jordan braced himself against her reaction and admitted, "A lot of people are pushing for it to be shut down."

With an embarrassed little shrug, Georgia said, "I understand." Then she moved away from him. "I need to get going. It's late and I'm tired and I've got some things to do when I get home."

He hated seeing her withdrawal. "Georgia..." He was uncertain what to say. "I don't mean to hurt you."

"I know. But if I lose this job...I don't know where I'll be able to make as much money." She went about pulling on her shoes and slipping on her lightweight jacket. Jordan watched her movements with barely leashed possessiveness.

"You could work for me." He didn't really need more help, but he'd hire her in a heartbeat. In fact, he really liked the idea once he said it out loud.

Her eyes looked silver rather than gray in the dim light. "I'm sure Elizabeth will have something to say about that."

"She'd be glad for the help."

"Nonsense. You bragged to me yourself that she keeps everything running smoothly." With her purse and her bag hanging from her shoulder, Georgia clasped her hands together and silently requested that he stop blocking the door.

Even in his wildest dreams, Jordan couldn't have imagined how badly he'd dread leaving a damn closet. But he had no reason to keep her inside now that she was ready to go. He opened the door and stepped out. "I'll walk you to your car."

"I would object, but I suppose you'd start insisting?" In spite of all that had just happened, she sounded shyly teasing, and Jordan smiled in relief.

"Of course."

Because they were looking at each other rather than where they walked, they almost bumped into Honey and Elizabeth.

"Hey," Elizabeth said. "Great show, Georgia!"

Jordan gaped at them. His sisters-in-law? In The Swine? He said, "Uh…"

Honey pulled Georgia—who was speechless with astonishment—into a tight hug. "I had no idea you were so talented. And I love the costume!" In an audible whisper, she said, "No one would ever guess you'd had two kids. You looked fantastic." Then in a further confidence, she added, "Sawyer would keel over dead if I wore anything that sexy."

Elizabeth laughed. "Gabe would probably faint. *After.*"

"After?" Georgia asked, still looking bewildered.

"Yeah, after he wore himself out." She chuckled. "The man does like to—"

Jordan said again, "Uh…"

"Oh, relax, Jordan," Honey told him, patting at his chest. The touch didn't feel at all the same as when Georgia did it.

He caught Honey's hand and gathered together his wits. "What are you two doing here?"

In unison, they said, "We came to watch Georgia dance."

"I...I didn't see you," Georgia told them, glancing nervously at Jordan.

Jordan felt poleaxed. When his brothers found out, there'd be hell to pay and somehow he'd probably get blamed. "Neither did I."

"Well, we didn't just sit out in the open, silly." Honey looked at him as though he should have figured that one out on his own. "We didn't want to make Georgia nervous. We were in the back corner booth. The bouncer—what was his name, Elizabeth?"

Elizabeth smiled. "Gus."

"Yes, Gus made sure no one bothered us."

Jordan glanced at the big no-neck ape who he'd tangled with that first night, and got a sharp nod. Jordan nodded in return. Good grief.

"Anyway," Honey said, waving away the remainder of that topic, "I was positively amazed how well you dance. It's incredible. Even when Jordan fell off his chair, you barely missed a beat."

Elizabeth snickered.

His face red and his temper on the rise, Jordan asked, "Where does Sawyer think you are?"

"At the movies."

His grin wasn't nice. "Not for long."

Honey gasped. "Don't you dare tell! You know he'll have a fit."

"Rightfully so."

Elizabeth shrugged. "I don't care if you tell. Gabe's not my boss."

Honey considered that, then shrugged, too. "Well, Sawyer's not my boss, either, but he is somewhat overprotective."

"Somewhat? Ha!" Elizabeth flipped her long red

hair over her shoulder then leaned toward Georgia. "Before you get too involved with this family, you should know that they're autocrats. All in different ways, of course, but they sure do like to hover, if you know what I mean."

Jordan couldn't wait to deliver Elizabeth back to Gabe. "I do *not* hover."

Elizabeth raised an auburn brow and gave a pointed look at Jordan's arm squeezing Georgia's shoulders.

Muttering to himself, he asked, "Instead of debating this now, why don't we get the hell out of here? Bill's not too happy with me tonight anyway."

"He's not?" asked Georgia.

Jordan didn't want to explain exactly what her boss had said about a drinking limit, or how Jordan had reacted to his apathy. Luckily Honey saved him.

"He's a smarmy one, isn't he?" Honey asked.

Jordan stopped dead in midstep. In lethal tones, he asked, "Did he say something to you? Did he insult you?"

Both Honey and Elizabeth rushed to reassure him, patting his chest and shaking their heads. "No, of course not. He just looks like a weasel."

Georgia laughed. She looked at each of them, saw that they had no idea what she found humorous, and laughed some more. Jordan smiled, too. The ways that she affected him were numerous. Georgia breathed and he got aroused. But what her laughter did to him was enough to cause spontaneous combustion.

Still chuckling, she said, "I really do like your family, Jordan."

Elizabeth and Honey grinned widely.

The moist night air was very refreshing after being in the stale bar. A light breeze teased through the trees, ruffling Georgia's loose curls. She lifted her face into the breeze, breathing deeply. Jordan watched her, wanting her more than ever.

When they reached the parked cars, he played the consummate gentleman. He opened car doors and kissed cheeks and when his sisters-in-law were finally ready to head home, he cautioned them to drive safely.

Elizabeth rolled her eyes. Honey told him to do the same. They waved to Georgia and drove off.

When Jordan looked down at Georgia, there was still a small, very sweet smile curving her mouth. He tipped up her chin with the side of his hand. "Do you know how badly I want to kiss you right now?"

"You're incorrigible."

"And you're breathless, which means you want me to kiss you, too. Don't you?"

"I'm breathless," she said somewhat smugly, "because Honey and Elizabeth were so complimentary. It's been a long long time since anyone praised me for my dancing skills. And no, don't you dare say anything. The way men view what I do on stage has nothing to do with my actual talent."

Jordan blinked at her. An idea bloomed in his mind, growing, gaining momentum. "Where'd you learn to dance?"

"I took lessons as a child. All the other kids made fun of me for it, but I loved it. I've always enjoyed moving to the music. By the time I was a teenager, I was helping to teach the rest of the class. It's something that's always come naturally to me."

Jordan caught her shoulders and pulled her to her tiptoes. He kissed her soundly before she could object. For the first time since meeting her he felt like he had the upper hand. He could help her while helping himself to get closer to her. He pulled Georgia into his arms and spun her around, lifting her off her feet.

Georgia laughed in surprise while clinging to his shoulders. "What are you doing?"

"Dancing with you." She started to say something more, but he stopped and asked, "You won't forget about this weekend, right? The cookout? Honey has been planning it all month and the kids are looking forward to it. Sawyer has promised to make them his famous fruit salad with melon balls—kids love melon balls—and Casey intends to take them boating."

She ducked her head and said, "We'll be there."

Tipping her chin once again, Jordan asked, "You don't sound very happy about it. What's wrong?"

She shook her head, refusing to answer. But then, he didn't really need her to. He knew she resisted their growing closeness and the need that got harder and harder to ignore. She was afraid if she relied on him, he might let her down. Jordan smiled, remembering that she wanted options.

He'd start working on that first thing in the morning.

9

THE KITCHEN was filled to overflowing with meddling relatives when Jordan walked in for breakfast. Even though Morgan and Misty now lived up on the hill, they often came down for breakfast. Honey insisted on it. And since Gabe and Elizabeth were still living downstairs in the renovated basement of the big house, they were always there in the mornings, too. The women generally helped each other out, cooking, watching babies, laughing and providing a nice feminine touch to what used to be a totally masculine gathering.

Casey, he noted, wallowed in all the attention. The women doted on him shamefully.

Jordan saw everyone look up when he closed the kitchen door. His own apartments were over the garage, converted years ago when he realized he was a little different than the others, that he wanted and needed more privacy than they did. "Morning."

Morgan, with his daughter Amber perched on his lap, leaned back and grinned. "I hear you're checking into property around town. You thinking of moving?"

"No!" Honey put down the spatula she'd been using to turn eggs and turned to Jordan with a horrified expression. "It's bad enough that Gabe and Elizabeth are planning to move. I *like* having you all here!"

Misty picked up the spatula and took over for her sister. "He's been looking at warehouses, not homes."

"Oh." Honey seemed so relieved that Sawyer walked up to her, put his arms around her from behind and began kissing her nape.

"You can't keep them all underfoot forever, sweetie."

She looked dreamy for a moment—a common occurrence when Sawyer kissed her or touched her—then scowled at him over her shoulder. "Don't say that. You'll have them thinking we want them to leave."

"My brothers know they're always welcome."

"And their wives."

Sawyer nodded. "I think I hear Shohn."

He left the room, oblivious to Casey's chuckles. "How the heck does he hear Shohn," Casey asked, "when no one else does? What'd the baby do? Burp?"

Everyone laughed except Honey. She, being as attuned to the baby as her husband, said matter-of-factly, "No, he yawned."

Morgan brought the conversation back around just as Jordan sprawled into his seat. "So why are you checking out warehouses?"

Jordan tried to stare him down before everyone started questioning him, but it didn't work. Amber reached up and pulled on her daddy's nose, and Jordan had to smile. He adored kids and Amber was a real cutie. Luckily, she looked just like her mother.

He wondered how they'd found out about his property inquiries so soon. Granted, he'd started checking into it yesterday morning, right after the idea had come to him the night before. But he'd barely called five places. Half the time he thought his family had radar.

Misty, long since recovered from her bout with the flu, jumped in, saying, "According to what Honey and Elizabeth told me about Georgia's talent, I bet he's thinking of putting together a dance studio. Buckhorn doesn't have anything like that, you know. A little culture wouldn't hurt anyone."

If he'd been prepared, if he'd had any forewarning at all that Misty might guess so close to the truth, Jordan could have blustered his way out of it. But he didn't. He simply stared, in awe of Misty's ability.

She felt him looking at her and glanced back. "What? Am I right?"

Morgan laughed. "Damn, you're good, sweetheart! And Jordan, I personally think it's a helluva idea."

"Helluva idea," Amber said, and Morgan quickly tried to hush her, but not quick enough. Misty glared at him with one of her you're-in-trouble looks.

"Amber, sweetie," Misty said, "Daddy's got a nasty mouth and says things he shouldn't. You can't always copy him or people will say you have a nasty mouth, too."

Amber pursed her cute little rosebud mouth and nodded. "Daddy's nasty."

"That's right." Misty kissed her daughter, who kissed her nasty daddy, just to make him stop looking so guilty.

Sawyer walked back in with Shohn on his shoulder. The baby still looked sleepy and had a soft printed blanket clutched in his chubby fist.

Honey said immediately, "Jordan is going to buy Georgia a dance studio."

Sawyer drew up short. "He's going to what?"

Jordan leaned forward, put his head on the table, and covered it with his arms. Amber patted his ear.

"A dance studio?"

"Yes." Honey took the baby and snuggled him close. "Georgia would be a wonderful dance instructor."

"How do you know?" Jordan asked, his voice muffled because he hadn't sat up yet.

A heavy pause filled the air. Everyone looked at Jordan. He sighed and propped his head up on his fist. "What makes you think she'd be a good instructor?"

Knowing his ploy, Honey lifted her chin and said, "Because I watched her dance two nights ago, as you very well know."

Jordan couldn't have been more amazed by her admission than if she'd thrown an egg at him. "You told him?"

She nodded. He glanced at Elizabeth who sat in Gabe's lap. "Of course we told."

Jordan stared at his brothers' red faces. "And neither of you are angry?"

"Damn right I'm angry," Sawyer admitted. "I told her she should have told me if she'd wanted to go and I would have taken her."

"Damn right," Amber said. When Sawyer groaned, she asked, "Unca Sawyer nasty, too?"

"Yeah," Morgan answered. "Nastier than me." He kissed Amber's belly and made her laugh.

Gabe made a face. "I had fully intended to impress upon Elizabeth the error of her ways, but it didn't work out quite as I had intended."

Morgan covered Amber's ears and said with remorse, "I know what you mean. You plan on giving a woman a good swat, but once you've got her pants off, you forget what you're doing."

Misty pinched Morgan for that bit of impertinence. Elizabeth just laughed, knowing it was all bluster. It was the truth not a one of them would ever lay a harsh hand on a female and their wives more than understood that.

Jordan laughed. God, he loved the lot of them. They were all nuts and overbearing and intrusive, and he had no idea what he'd do without them. The phone rang so he decided to excuse himself from the chaos.

He went into the family room and when he picked up the receiver and said, "Hello," he heard a long pause before his mother asked, "What's wrong?"

Jordan stared at the phone. "Mother?"

"Of course it's your mother. Now tell me what's wrong."

Of course it's your mother? Jordan held the receiver away from his ear to stare at it. His mother and Brett now lived in Florida. She'd called last week, but he'd been at Georgia's and missed her.

Because he wasn't sure how much she knew, Jordan hedged. "What makes you think anything's wrong?" Though he'd just been entertaining softer thoughts about his family, he now considered knocking all their heads together. If one of his damn brothers had been tattling, upsetting their mother, he wouldn't be pleased.

"I can hear it in your voice," she explained. "You've always had the most betraying voice. Even when you were a baby, I could tell by your gurgles what you were thinking and feeling."

Jordan dropped onto the edge of the couch and without giving himself time to plan out his reply, he said, "I think I'm in love."

Another pause, then softly: "Will you tell me about her?"

Even as he considered his words, Jordan smiled. "She's beautiful."

"Of course."

"But that's not what got to me." He frowned. "She has two kids. Lisa, six and Adam, four. They're incredible."

There was a smug note in his mother's voice when she said, "Then obviously *she's* incredible."

"She is. And gutsy. She's made a few mistakes, I guess. And..." Jordan hesitated. "In a lot of ways, she's like you."

Another pause. "How's that?"

Jordan looked toward the doorway, saw no one was lurking, and said, "She'll do anything necessary to see that her kids are taken care of."

His mother laughed. "What in the world did I ever do to warrant that comment? You make it sound like I worked in the coal mines to feed you or something."

Jordan considered all the things she had done, the sacrifices she'd made, how hard she'd always worked to make them happy. But the one thing that really stood out in his mind, the one thing he'd always hated, slipped out without his permission. "You married my father," he said, "hoping to make a complete home for Sawyer and Morgan."

"Jordan!" She sounded incredulous that he'd come to such a conclusion. "I married your father because I loved him!"

Jordan heard a muffled shout in the background and his mother said, "No Brett, it's not Gabe. It's Jordan." And then: "Yes, I can see how you made that assumption."

Jordan chuckled. He could just imagine what Brett, Gabe's father, was thinking right now. "Tell Brett I said 'hi.'"

"Later. Right now I have something that I want you to understand. Do you have your listening ears on, Jordan?"

"My listening ears?" She hadn't used that term on him since before he'd become a teen.

"Don't get smart, son. Just pay attention."

He grinned even as he said, "Yes, ma'am."

"I have never regretted marrying your father. How could I when I have you?"

"He was a damn drunk."

"He was human. He made mistakes and in my mind, he's paid dearly for them. He lost me, and he lost all of you. Surely there couldn't have been a worse penalty."

Jordan gripped the receiver hard. "He was irresponsible, selfish—"

"No, sweetheart, he was just an alcoholic." She sighed, then continued. "We humans are prone to screwing up our lives on occasion. Most of the time we're given the chance to make amends. Your father was a wonderful man when I met him. Things happened that he couldn't deal with, and he...well, he wasn't strong enough to cope. If you ever get to meet him, I hope you keep that in mind."

Jordan didn't want to meet him, ever. But to appease his mother, he said, "I'll think on it."

"Now tell me about this young lady you're going to marry."

He choked on his own indrawn breath. "I didn't say anything about marrying her! I haven't even known her that long. It's just..."

"It's just that you love her. So why wait?"

"Well, one good reason might be that she doesn't want to marry me. In fact, she doesn't even want to see me."

"That's ridiculous! Why wouldn't she? There's no finer man than you."

Jordan got an evil grin when he said, "I'll tell the others you said so."

Laughing, his mother replied, "You're all equally fine men. And I can tell them myself this evening."

"There's no need to call back. Everyone's here for breakfast."

"That's not what I meant. Brett and I are flying in tonight. We should make it to the house by about five."

Jordan froze. "You're coming here? Tonight?"

"Now, Jordan, if I didn't know better, I'd say you didn't want to see me."

Jordan quickly reassured her otherwise. But in his mind, he was thinking of the cookout, the fact that Georgia would be there with her kids. He'd hoped to tell her about the studio, but until he knew for certain that there was a building that'd work, he didn't want to mention it.

His mother again told him that she loved him, and Jordan reciprocated. It'd be good to see her, and the babies would love it, not to mention how Casey would feel. But with his mother there, he didn't know if he'd be able to get a single moment alone with Georgia.

And that's what he wanted, because he was through with waiting. He'd planned to cement their relationship in the oldest way known to mankind.

Now that he'd seen firsthand how she responded to him, he knew it would be so damn good, so explosive, she'd never be able to deny him again.

RUTH WAS in the kitchen baking when Georgia walked in. She paused, watching her mother for a moment before announcing herself. Ruth looked pretty in a matching nightgown and robe decorated with small sprigs of yellow flowers. Her light brown hair, now slightly streaked with gray, was twisted at the back of her head in a loose knot. She was humming as she put a new sheet of cookies in the oven.

"Morning, Mom."

Ruth turned with a smile and then went to Georgia to kiss her cheek. "You're up early!"

Georgia grinned. "So are you. And baking already?" She made a beeline for the coffeepot, as usual. Now, whenever she drank a cup, she thought of Jordan—and remembered everything he'd made her feel.

"I wanted to bring something to the cookout today. I'm looking forward to it."

Georgia's heart swelled. The kids had talked about little else for the past few days and her mother's eyes glowed with just the mention of the gathering. Georgia hadn't realized how isolated, how withdrawn from society she'd kept them all. Between working so much, both at the bar and on the house, there'd been little time for playing. It seemed every day she found another way that she'd failed the ones she loved most.

"I'm sorry. I hadn't thought about how lonely you might have been."

Ruth shook her head. "Or how lonely *you've* been?"

She started to deny that, but Ruth took her coffee cup and set it aside, then clasped both of Georgia's hands and squeezed them. "Georgia, it's okay to admit it, you know." Her mother met her gaze squarely and stated, "It's also okay to want a man."

"Mother!" Georgia felt a hot blush begin creeping up her neck.

"Oh, don't give me that tone." Ruth paid no heed to her daughter's embarrassment. "I'm older, not dead. I know how it is. And Jordan is...well, he's a potent male. Personally I think you're downright foolish to keep putting him off."

Georgia thought she might fall through the floor with her mother's words. "He *is* potent, and that's what scares me." In a softer voice, she admitted, "It'd be so easy to love him."

"So?" Ruth sounded totally unconcerned with her plight. "The kids and I love him, so you might as well, too."

Georgia shook her head. "It isn't that easy, Mom. I thought I loved Dennis—"

"You did love Dennis. And I think he honestly loved you. He was just young, Georgia. Young and foolish." Ruth hesitated, then said, "Let's sit down. I want to tell you something."

Georgia agreed, but she also snatched back her coffee cup. No way could she handle all this without some caffeine. Luckily the kids were still sleeping soundly, giving them some quiet time alone.

As Georgia refilled her cup, she looked around her

home. Everything was in order now. Oh, there were still plenty of repairs to be made, but nothing crucial. She could finally see the end of the tunnel. And beyond the material things, her children were more lively than they'd ever been. They'd flourished under all the added attention from Jordan and his family.

Morgan had dubbed them "official deputies" and given them both badges to wear. Casey took them swimming and boating and taught them both how to fish. Saywer had let them listen to their own heartbeats with his stethoscope. The women had praised Lisa for helping with the babies and had convinced Adam that he was the handsomest guy in Buckhorn, even more so than Gabe—which made her shy son start strutting.

And Jordan...Georgia sighed just thinking about him. It amazed her that one man could truly be so wonderful. He'd gone with them to find salamanders in the woods behind the house. One day he had even paid them to help him at his office, though Georgia knew they'd been in the way more than not. Still, he never seemed to mind. They started the day talking about him, and often wanted to call him in the evening to tell him good-night.

"Georgia?"

She hadn't realized that she'd stopped in the middle of the floor and was just standing there. She looked at her mother, saw her caring and love and acceptance, and she burst into tears.

Ruth didn't cry with her. As she got out of her seat to embrace her daughter, she gave a sympathetic chuckle. "Love is the damndest thing, isn't it?"

Georgia tried to mop her eyes and hold on to her

coffee at the same time. "I don't know what I'm going to do."

"You're going to tell him." Ruth held her away so she could see her face, and nodded when Georgia shook her head. "Sweetheart, don't make the same mistakes I made. Don't waste your time being afraid. Sometimes you just have to take a few chances, and I think Jordan's worth the risk, don't you?"

With a shuddering breath, Georgia reached for a napkin off the counter and blew her nose. She whispered, "He's never said anything about loving me."

"So? Your father dutifully told me every night that he loved me. But it would have meant so much more if he'd shown me instead. If he'd cared when I was tired or sick. If he'd held me when I was upset."

Georgia stared at her mother. *If he'd given her foot rubs and held her when she was afraid and loved her children....* Her father had never really loved her, not the way she loved Adam and Lisa.

As if she'd read her thoughts, Ruth nodded. "Jordan has shown you that he cares in more ways than I can count."

"Oh, God." Her mother was right. From the moment she'd met Jordan, she'd known he was different. True, he was pushy and arrogant and determined—but according to his family, he only behaved that way when he really cared about something. Or someone. She didn't want to rely on him, but...maybe it would be okay. Maybe depending on him to share with her, to give and let her give, too, wouldn't be so bad. If she could only balance her independence against what he made her feel....

But she knew she'd always hate herself if she didn't at least give him a chance. "I'll tell him today."

Ruth laughed out loud. "That's wonderful!" She hugged Georgia again before gently pushing her into a seat at the table. "Now, how about a cookie to celebrate?"

From the doorway, Adam and Lisa said, "I want one, too!" and as Georgia opened her arms to her children, still sleepy warm from their beds, she thought that she had to be the luckiest woman alive. Perhaps after today, she'd also be the most fulfilled.

JORDAN HEARD her car pull up and walked around to the front of the house. People had been arriving all afternoon, and he'd been anxiously waiting for her. He'd found a studio, and he could barely wait to discover her reaction to that.

The moment they saw him, Adam and Lisa jumped out and came running, followed by Ruth. Jordan was barely able to swallow down his emotion as he embraced both children. They chatted ninety miles a minute, telling him about all the cookies their grandma had made and about the pictures they'd colored for him to decorate his office, and about a frog they'd found in the backyard.

"Jus' like you tol' us to, we played with it and then turned it loose."

Jordan stroked Adam's downy hair, warmed by the sun. "I'm sure the frog appreciates it. They're not meant to be pets."

Lisa nodded. "We remembered." Then she leaned forward to whisper, "'Sides, Grandma hates frogs."

Jordan was still chuckling when Ruth and Georgia

reached his side. Ruth gave him a hug, though Georgia looked shyly away, prompting him to curious speculation. Following the lead her mother and children had set, Jordan pulled Georgia close for a hug. To his surprise, she briefly nuzzled her nose into his throat and sighed.

Just that easily, he was aroused. Of course, he stayed semiaroused around her anyway.

Trying to discern her mood, Jordan studied her and only vaguely heard Ruth announce that she and the kids were taking the cookies to Honey. Georgia waited until she'd gone, then licked her lips in a show of nervousness.

Jordan touched her hair, teased by the warm afternoon breeze. He loved how the golden-brown curls framed her face and how the sunlight glinted in them. "Georgia?" His voice was husky, affected by more than his sexual need of her. He wanted her, all of her. Forever. "Is something wrong?"

He took her arm and started her toward the back of the house where everyone was gathered. He could feel the tension emanating from her and sought to make her more at ease by rubbing her back.

Her eyes closed and she moaned softly, then suddenly blurted, "I have something I want to tell you."

Jordan tensed. He could tell by her expression that she wasn't completely comfortable with what she had to say. If she thought to try pulling away from him, after they were finally getting so close, she could damn well think again. He took her hand in his and laced their fingers together. Jordan could hear the others chatting in the backyard as they rounded the house, though Georgia seemed oblivious.

"I've been going over everything you said." She peeked a look at him, then frowned in concentration. "That last night at the bar, I mean."

Jordan nodded. "I want to talk about that, too." He now had options for her, viable options. He hoped she'd be pleased.

She stared at him in sudden horror. "You've changed your mind? You don't want me anymore?"

"*What?*" Jordan jerked around to stare at her. "No," he said, his frown deepening. "Hell, no. Where'd you get that crazy idea?"

"I thought—" She shook her head and started walking again. "I thought maybe, because I pushed so hard, you'd decided to leave me alone now."

"Georgia." How could she possibly think such a thing? Leave her alone? He couldn't even stop thinking about her, so how would he keep away?

They had just stepped into the backyard when she drew a deep breath and said, "That's good, because...I want you, too." She looked up at him, her eyes so pale in the sunlight. "Jordan, I don't think I've ever wanted any man as much as I want you. What...what you did to me the other night? That was wonderful and I loved it. I haven't been able to think of much else. But I want more than that." She stared him right in the eyes and whispered, "I want to feel you inside me and I want to watch your face when you come, and I want to hear your voice and hold you. I want that so badly I can't stand it anymore."

Jordan sucked in a huge breath of air, but it didn't help. Just that quickly he had an erection that threatened the seams of his jeans. Every muscle in his body shook.

And then the sound of conversation intruded and he looked around, seeing himself surrounded by family and neighbors. Luckily no one was paying them any attention.

He groaned aloud. Georgia finally admitted to wanting him, and there wasn't an ounce of privacy to be found. "Sweetheart, you really know how to make a man crazy."

She stared up at him, her eyes full of questions. And invitation. "It's fair. You've certainly made me nuts." She reached up and touched his face. "Can I ask you something?"

Jordan put his arm around her and led her to the side of the yard, as far away from the others as he dared to go without drawing a lot of attention. "You can ask me anything, Georgia. Don't ever forget that."

Her smile was so sweet and gentle. He loved her mouth. Damn, how he loved her mouth.

"If," she said, looking uncertain once again, "I didn't want to be involved with you. If I made it clear that I had no feelings for you at all—"

"Then I'd respect your wishes, even if it killed me."

She went on tiptoe to give him a quick kiss. "I already knew that. You're not a man to ever force a woman in any way."

Jordan laughed at her assumptions. "I'd do my damndest first to convince you."

"You already have. Done your damndest *and* convinced me. But you're such a seducer with that sexy voice—" she touched his mouth with one fingertip "—it wasn't that hard."

The way she touched him, how she looked at him,

took him to the edge. In a rasp, he said, "Speak for yourself."

She understood his meaning and glanced down at his fly. "Oh." Warmth colored her cheekbones, making him nuts, but when he went to kiss her, she said, "Jordan, it was something else I was going to ask."

"Tell me."

"If we had no personal relationship, would you still want to see my kids? Or would you suddenly disappear from their lives?"

Jordan didn't give a damn if everyone in Buckhorn saw him. He cupped her face in his hands and took her mouth in a kiss meant to offer reassurance and so much more. When he lifted away, she clung to him, as unconcerned with their audience as he was. "I love your kids, sweetheart. I'd never do that to them."

Tears glistened on her lashes. "That's what I thought."

Jordan knew what she was getting at. Their own father had walked away, just as his had. For whatever reason, her ex had been able to give up his own two offspring, never knowing if they were all right, if they needed him or not.

But Jordan was different. He'd never before realized exactly how different until that moment. "I used to worry about my father," he said. "Not about his well-being, but whether or not people would associate me with him. Like your ex-husband, he split after the divorce and no one has seen him since. Not a single phone call, not even a card. If I died, I'm not sure he'd know, or even care."

Jordan shrugged and admitted, "There've been times when I hated him because I felt so ashamed. Not because he wasn't here, but because my brothers had respectable, honorable, loving fathers and yet my father was a huge mistake."

His throat felt raw as he told her things he'd never said to another living soul. "I wanted to hold myself to a higher standard, to prove to myself and to everyone else that I was better than that, better than him."

Georgia put her arms around him and rested the side of her face on his chest. He cupped the back of her neck, tangling his fingers in her soft curls.

He smiled when she said, "You're the best person I've ever met." But then she added, "You make me feel so inferior."

Jordan abruptly pushed her back so he could scowl into her face. "What the hell are you talking about?"

She lifted her shoulders in a slow shrug. "I know it probably bothers you to want me. I got pregnant at sixteen, I've already been divorced and I dance in a bar." Her smile was sad and fleeting. "I'm hardly anybody's idea of a 'higher standard.'"

Rage washed over him, making him break out in a sweat. His vision narrowed to her face, a face he loved. He gave her a quick, sharp shake. "Don't you *ever* say anything like that again!"

"Jordan!" She glanced around, reminding him that they weren't alone. "Someone will hear you."

It took all his concentration to lower his voice, to temper his fury. Tears filled her eyes again, slicing into him like the sharpest blade. It was her vulnerability that gained him some control. He pulled her into his chest and held her tight. "I never thought," he whispered against her forehead, "that I'd meet someone as beautiful as you. Do you know what I see when I look at you, Georgia?"

She shook her head.

"I see a woman who will do anything she has to in order to take care of the people who depend on her. A woman with enough strength and courage and honor to beat the odds, and still be so incredibly sweet that it breaks my heart just to look at her."

Georgia's self-conscious laugh teased along his senses. He felt her wipe her eyes on his shirt and wished he was alone with her. She filled him with lust, broke his heart with her gentleness and humbled him with her strength.

"You make me sound like a conquering Amazon," she whispered.

He put his mouth close to her ear. "From the moment I saw you," he breathed, relishing her scent and her softness, "I was so hot to have you I nearly ground my teeth into powder. That's never happened to me before. I stay so aroused I ache, but I only want you."

Her hands fisted in his shirt. "Me, too. I want you so much, it scares me."

He didn't want her to fear him, but he'd explain that to her later. "I think you're the sexiest woman I've ever met. And the more I got to know you, the worse it became, because your sexiness is earthy. It isn't just about your gorgeous body, or the way you move or how you look at me. It's you. Everything about you, Georgia. Do you understand?"

She nodded. "All right."

Jordan suddenly felt someone behind him. He jerked around and found Morgan and Gabe both breathing down his neck.

"Hey," Morgan said, as if he hadn't just intruded. "You two are embarrassing everyone, me included. Why don't you find a room somewhere?"

Gabe shoved Morgan. "You're so crude." Then to Georgia: "Put him out of his misery, sweetheart. Jordan isn't used to this kind of excitement. Sawyer says it isn't good for his heart."

Georgia covered her face and laughed. Jordan thought about tossing his brothers into the lake. But then Morgan whispered, "You know, the gazebo is real private. Everyone is getting ready to eat and I can keep the kids occupied if you two want to go...talk things over."

Jordan looped his arm around Georgia and pulled her to his side. He peered around the yard. Zenny and Walt and Newton waved to them. Georgia groaned, but waved back. Howard and Jesse were arguing—as usual.

Morgan's enormous dog, Godzilla, had the kids well occupied. Lisa, Adam and Amber were all petting him and Godzilla rested on his back in doggy bliss, his tongue hanging out of the side of his mouth. Godzilla looked more like the missing link than a pet, but he was about the sweetest creature Jordan had ever seen. Even Honey's calico cat liked the dog. She sat next to Lisa, getting her own pet every now and then and rubbing her head against Godzilla's hip.

"Will you look at my mother?" Georgia said in awe.

Jordan followed the direction of Georgia's gaze and found Ruth in animated conversation with Misty's and Honey's bachelor father. Damned if there wasn't a bright blush on her face, too. Well, well, Jordan thought. He wasn't crazy about the man, despite how he'd softened since his daughters had joined the family, but whatever he said to Ruth must have been complimentary because she hadn't stopped smiling once.

He heard a laugh and noticed Casey was sitting beneath a shade tree, surrounded by female admirers. Gabe nodded toward Casey, chuckling. "They've been after him all day. He can't get himself a cola without them all trailing behind."

Even as Gabe spoke, Emma walked up to group. She wore another halter top that showed more than it concealed and shorts that should have been illegal. She was barefoot, carrying her sandals, and Casey made an obvious point of not looking at her, at completely ignoring her existence—until two of the girls said something obviously snide. Emma, head bowed, started to walk away and within two heartbeats Casey was at her side. They appeared to disagree on something for just a moment, then Casey shook his head, slung his arm around her shoulders, and practically dragged her off.

A lot of feminine complaints ensued as Casey and Emma disappeared around the side of the house.

Georgia sighed. "I really adore your nephew."

Morgan laughed. "We're rather fond of him, too." Under his breath he added, "But what the hell is he up to?"

"You two should get going," Gabe said. "But I'd take the long route if I was you. Casey's not the only one with disgruntled females hunting for him."

Georgia frowned over that, looking around the yard with an evil glint in her eyes. Jordan appreciated her mild show of jealousy; she'd admitted to wanting him and now she was acting possessive. All he needed was a quiet spot to show her how much he cared.

Morgan suddenly laughed. "Too late. You should have fled when you had the chance."

"What are you talking about?" Jordan demanded, not in the least amused by the possibility of yet another delay.

"She's here." Morgan tipped his head toward the backdoor of the house. "And you know there's no way in hell she'll let you slink away."

Georgia's frown turned ferocious. "She *who?*"

Gabe, too, looked at the house, then started to laugh. "Our mother. Prepare yourself, Georgia, she's making a beeline this way."

All three brothers smiled and started forward; Jordan pulled Georgia along with him. They met Sawyer on the path and before Megan Kasper could descend off the back stoop, she was enveloped in masculine hugs that kept her completely off her feet for a good five minutes.

10

"YOUR CHILDREN are wonderful."

Georgia smiled at Megan as she stroked Lisa's hair. "Thank you."

Lisa sent Megan a big grin, worshiping her. Of course, she and Adam had both been amazed by this tiny woman who ruled her gigantic sons with an iron fist. The men jumped at her slightest whisper, and did so with grins on their faces.

Georgia had heard so many stories about Megan's stubbornness, her strong will, she'd certainly expected someone...bigger. But while Megan was small in stature, she had an enormous smile and an innate gentleness and she loved to laugh.

It tickled Georgia to see how her sons fawned over her. When Megan had first arrived several hours ago, she'd been passed from one strong set of arms to another. How such a small woman could mother such colossal men was beyond her. When one of the neighbors had commented on it with a smile, another had said that Megan always gravitated to the "big guys." Seeing her husband, Georgia understood.

Brett Kasper had stood there looking pleased and smug and adoring over everything Megan did. He resembled his son Gabe quite a bit, in that they were both drop-dead gorgeous, they both liked to pet on their wives, and they were both strongly built. Once the brothers had finished with Megan, Brett had been treated to a round of bear hugs himself, with no preferences shown. He was, obviously, very well loved.

"I'm going to skin Casey when he gets here."

Georgia laughed at that, knowing Megan was anxious to see him again. Georgia leaned forward and said, "He went off with a girl."

"I never doubted it for a moment." Megan frowned at Jordan, sitting beside her in a lawn chair, and said, "He's far too much like his uncles *not* to be with a female."

Lisa thought that was funny and giggled, but when she saw Adam go by chasing the dog, she ran after them. Georgia watched her go, feeling so incredibly at peace.

Jordan shrugged. "He's a little like Gabe, with the girls after him. And a little like Sawyer, being so compassionate. I'm just not sure what's motivating him today." As he spoke, he lifted one of Georgia's feet, pulled off her sandal, and started another foot rub. She gawked at him, but Megan only smiled and Jordan didn't even seem aware of what he was doing. "I think Emma has him on the run."

Both Megan and Jordan ignored Georgia's struggle to retrieve her foot. *"Jordan..."*

He smiled at her, then said to his mother, "Georgia's a dancer, you know. In high heels."

"Ah." Megan did her best to hide her amusement as Jordan caught her other foot also. "I suppose that explains it."

Georgia thought she might die of embarrassment, but instead she ended up groaning. Everyone talked about Jordan's magical voice; why hadn't anyone warned her about his magical hands?

Megan stood. "I see Ruth and Misty calling the kids in. Sounds like they're going to make popcorn. I think I'll help."

Sure enough, Amber led the way with Lisa and Adam following, trailed by the dog and cat. Misty held Shohn in her arms while Ruth kept the door open for the parade. Georgia was amazed at how the kids were so accepted by everyone. They didn't deliberately take turns that she'd noticed, but somehow it worked out that way. Earlier she and Jordan had taken them all on an expedition to the lake where they'd lifted stones along the shore and found not only crawdads, but minnows and rock bass. Amber, strangely enough, had been the most daring at grabbing for the creepy-crawly creatures. But then Jordan explained that she'd been in or near the water since her birth, thanks to Gabe. Adam and Lisa professed to love it, too, so Jordan had promised to get Gabe to take them to the dam very soon.

They were all so giving and so accepting. Her children had found a family here. And that made her full to bursting with happiness.

Since Georgia couldn't stand, given that Jordan had both her feet held firmly in his lap, Megan bent down to her instead. After a tight hug and a kiss on the cheek, she said, "I'll be in town for awhile this trip. Do you think we could get together for lunch or something? I'd love to visit more."

Georgia glanced at Jordan, saw his small smile, and agreed. "I'd enjoy that. Thank you."

Next Megan clasped Jordan's face between her hands and said, "I love seeing you so happy."

Jordan chuckled. "I'm rather fond of the situation myself."

She kissed him soundly and then took herself off. She'd barely gone ten feet when a rubber-tipped dart hit her in the backside. Megan jumped, whipped around, saw Gabe hiding behind a tree and started after him. Gabe ran for his life as Morgan and Sawyer, standing together at the back door, doubled over in laughter.

Georgia couldn't help but laugh, too. Then she looked up and locked gazes with Jordan. He looked...serious.

"Jordan?"

His fingers continued to work over her feet, only now his touch felt more sexual, more exciting. She let out a small, breathy moan, imagining those hands in other places.

"Do you know," he whispered, his eyes so hot she felt scorched, "that I'm about to die from unsated lust? I want you so bad right now I'm close to—"

"Ho!" Sawyer slapped him on the back, nearly knocking Jordan out of his lawn chair. "Hold that thought until I'm a safe distance away."

Jordan's growl was feral. "*Damn it*, will you guys stop sneaking up on me!"

Sawyer bit back a laugh. "Mom has decided to do a sleepover, just like she used to when we were young." In a stage whisper he added, "It's possible she's hoping to give you a helping hand."

Then to Georgia, "Honey's already dragging the family-room furniture around, making space for the tent, but Mom said she wants your permission to invite Adam and Lisa to spend the night, too."

Jordan closed his eyes and ignored Sawyer.

Georgia, a bit shaken by the interruption and her own repressed desire, said dumbly, "A tent?"

"Yeah. Kids love making tents out of blankets and stuff. They'll sleep on the floor and Mom and Brett will sleep on the couch." He shrugged. "It's her way of giving everyone a night off. Except me because Honey is still breast-feeding, but we're claiming tomorrow afternoon." He grinned shamelessly with that admission.

Jordan came to his feet in a rush, cupped the back of Georgia's head, and gave her a hard kiss. "Say yes."

She looked into his eyes, saw all the promise there, and nodded. "Yes."

Jordan's eyes flared with satisfaction. "Let's see if I can keep you in such an agreeable mood," he murmured.

Ten minutes later Georgia found herself being hustled across the yard to Jordan's apartments over the garage. Her kids had kissed her goodbye and goodnight without a qualm. They knew she'd be close if she was needed. Ruth had been invited to 'camp out' with them and had accepted, especially when Mr. Malone had done the same.

Jordan paused beside the steps leading to his front door.

"What is it?" Georgia asked, a little breathless from the idea of what they were about to do.

"I thought I heard something." Jordan frowned, looked around the yard, then shook his head. "Nevermind. It doesn't matter." He put his arm around her shoulders and together they practically ran up the steps. No sooner did Jordan have the door closed than Georgia found herself in his arms.

"God, I need you," he whispered and his rough velvet voice stroked over her as surely as his hands were doing. "Let me love you all night."

She would have said yes, but his mouth covered hers and his tongue thrust inside, hot and wet and hungry and all she could do was moan. Jordan must have understood; one of his large hands settled on her breast, softly kneading, and the other curved around the front of her thigh. He pressed into her, all hard, tensed muscles and trembling need. She felt his erection against her belly and rubbed herself against him.

In that instant, he lost it.

CASEY CHUCKLED as he saw the light go out in the rooms overhead. Jordan was a goner—and Casey had never seen him happier.

He was behind the garage in the darkest shadows, Emma clinging to his side. Very gently, he eased her away. "We should join the others."

"No." Her hand, so small and soft, stroked down his bare chest, but Casey caught it before she reached the fly to his jeans.

It took more control than he knew he had to turn her away. "Emma," he chided, and hopefully he was the only one who heard the shaking of his voice. He'd started out befriending her, but Emma wanted more. She was so blatant about it, so brazen, it was all he could do not to give in. But more than anything Emma needed a friend, not another conquest. And beyond that, Casey didn't share.

"Are you a virgin?" she taunted, and Casey laughed outright at her ploy.

"That," he said, flicking a finger over her soft cheek, "is none of your business."

She shook her head in wonder. "You're the only guy I know who wouldn't have denied it right away!"

"I'm not denying or confirming."

"I know, but most guys'd lie if they had to, rather than let a girl think—"

"What?" Casey cupped her face and despite his resolve, he kissed her. "I don't care what anyone thinks, Emma. You should know that by now. Besides, what I've done or with who isn't the point."

"No," she agreed, her tone sad. "It's what I've done, isn't it?"

He repeated his own thoughts out loud. "I don't share."

"What if I promised not to—"

"Shhh. Summer break is almost over and I'll be leaving for school. I won't be around, so there's no point in us even discussing this."

Big tears welled in her eyes, reflecting the moonlight, making his guts cramp. "I'm leaving too, Casey."

"And where do you think to go?"

"It doesn't matter." He could see her soft mouth trembling, could smell her sweet scent carried on the cool evening breeze. Boldly, she took his hand and pressed it to her breast. She was so damn soft.

With a muttered curse, Casey pulled her closer and kissed her again. It didn't matter, he promised himself, filling his hand with her firm breast, finding her nipple and stroking with his thumb. He was damned if he did, and damned if he didn't. And sometimes Emma was just too much temptation.

But it wouldn't change anything. He told her so in a muted whisper, and her only reply was a groan.

"I WANTED to go slow," Jordan ground out as he jerked Georgia's T-shirt high, pushed her bra aside and bared one breast. He had very large hands, but even for him she was lush and full. "I wanted to make this last."

"Don't you dare go slow," she gasped, and gripped his head as he closed his mouth over one taut straining nipple. "*Jordan.*"

He pulsed with incredible need, his heartbeat wild and uncontrolled. She tasted even better than he remembered, ripe and hot. With a low groan, she parted her thighs and she pushed against him, using her body to stroke his erection, her movements sinuous and graceful, making him think of all the fantasies he'd had when watching her dance.

He sucked her nipple deep, drawing on her while with his other hand he teased the crease of her behind. "Do you know what I want?" he growled, and switched to her other breast. The nipple he'd just abandoned was wet and so tight he ached just seeing it. He pinned her against the wall, knowing if he didn't slow her down he'd be gone in under three seconds.

Georgia gave a breathy, barely-there laugh. "It's obvious what you want." Her small hand pressed between them and curled around his hard-on. "This is a dead giveaway."

Jordan squeezed his eyes shut and concentrated on

holding back his orgasm. "Don't do that." He stepped away, putting an arm's length of distance between them, staring at her through a haze of lust. "I'm not sure how you manage it, but you set me off and I don't want to end this too quick. Not for me and not for you."

Georgia looked at him while using the wall for support. Her chest, bared from his petting, rose and fell with deep breaths and quick pants. Her legs were still parted, her hands flat on the wall beside her hips. She looked enticing and tempting and Jordan wanted to drag her down to the carpet and bury himself inside her until they both screamed with the pleasure of it.

Slowly she gathered her wits and a small, seductive smile curled that sexier-than-sin mouth. Her eyes were dark and inviting. "Tell me what you want, Jordan."

He didn't hesitate. "I want you to ride me. Hard. I want to lie on my back and watch you while you take your pleasure. I want to see all those sensual movements you make when you dance, only I want them for me and me alone." Her lips parted, her breath came faster. He added in a whisper, "And I want it all while I'm deep inside you."

She came away from the wall in a rush, grabbing him and kissing him—his mouth, his throat, his chest. Jordan palmed her backside, lifted her and started for his bedroom. When her legs wound around him he had to stop for just a moment and kiss her deeply, but he could feel his passions on the boiling point, ready to erupt.

He tripped over a pair of slacks on his bedroom

floor, stumbled to the bed and dropped there with Georgia still in his arms. "Don't move," he rasped.

She ignored him, grabbing his shirt and trying to yank it off him. He did that for her, then wrestled her own shirt over her head, leaving it and her bra twisted around her arms to try to hinder her movements just a bit.

"You're pushing me, sweetheart and I can't take it."

"Damn it, Jordan..." She struggled with the shirt and bra and by the time she had her arms free he'd already yanked her shorts and panties off.

Sitting back on his heels between her wide-spread legs, he whispered, "I could come just looking at you."

She moaned.

"Don't move now. I mean it." And before she could ignore that edict, he caught her hips in his hands, lifted her, and stroked with his tongue. She was already wet and hot and he grew voracious in his need to take as much of her as he could. "You taste so sweet."

Like a wild woman, she writhed and squirmed and cried out. Jordan loved it all, just as he loved her. His fingers bit deeply into her cheeks and he used his thumbs to open her further, stroking with his tongue and teasing with his teeth and breathing in her heady, musky scent.

His erection throbbed and strained against his fly, but he wanted her pleasure first because he wasn't at all certain how long he'd last once he got inside her. He'd meant to seduce her, but he forgot everything he knew about women and what they enjoyed. He acted solely on instinct, but it must have been enough. After several minutes of reacting to her moans and her small movements and her breathless encouragement, Jordan felt her climax start.

Her hips jerked, her thighs trembled and she groaned, long and low and real, pressing herself against his mouth to take everything he could give her. He held her closer, used his tongue to stroke her deeper, faster, and she came with all the energy she gave to her dance.

When she quieted, her harsh breathing the only sound in the room, Jordan rested his face against her thigh. Her completion, as if it had been his own, had helped to calm him. Idly, he traced his fingers over her slick flesh, her soft brown curls, making her twitch and moan.

He grinned. "This," he whispered, softly stroking her swollen folds before slowly, carefully pushing one finger deep, "was worth the wait."

She moved to his touch, lazy, sated movements. He loved seeing her spread out naked on his bed. When he pulled his fingers away, she heaved a long, shuddering sigh, and he decided he'd better not stall any longer or she was liable to fall asleep on him. And he knew firsthand how difficult it was to get her awake again.

Jordan stood beside the bed and stripped off his jeans. Georgia watched him through heavy, slumberous eyes—until he was naked. Then her cheekbones colored with renewed heat and her lips parted.

She took him completely off guard when she whispered, "I love you, Jordan."

An invisible fist squeezed his heart. Every bit of calm he'd just achieved shot out the ceiling.

He barely had the sense or patience to find a condom and put it on, especially when the second he sat on the mattress she pushed him to his back. Jordan dropped flat, more than willing to give her control. Without hesitation she straddled his hips. For a brief moment she cradled his testicles, testing his long-lost control, her small soft hand making him crazed. Holding back became torture, and he told her so.

She clasped his penis in her hand and thankfully guided him into her body.

Jordan watched as she slowly slid down to envelop him, and he groaned deeply. With only that initial stroke he felt his body drawing tight in prerelease. *"Georgia."*

She seated herself completely. He held her hips and pressed her down farther; he was so deep inside her, her inner muscles gripped him and she caught her breath on a gasp. When Jordan started to lift her away, unwilling to hurt her, she shook her head and braced her hands on his chest. Her gaze was cloudy with a mix of discomfort and incredible pleasure. "I want all of you."

Jordan locked his jaw and concentrated on not coming. Georgia didn't make it easy on him. At first, she held perfectly still and Jordan, teeth clenched and thighs tensed, did all he could to keep from rushing her.

Her thumbs found his nipples beneath his chest hair. "You are, without a doubt," she murmured, "the most gorgeous, sexy man I've ever seen."

His heels pressed into the mattress and his hands fisted in the sheets.

Her small palms, cool against his burning flesh,

coasted over his shoulders, down his biceps then to his abdomen. "You're all hard muscles and lean strength and I've wanted you since the first time I saw you in the audience."

Jordan felt himself jerking, knew the end was near for him. "Move, damn it. *Move.*"

With a feminine laugh of sheer power, she did as he asked, lifting with torturous slowness, then dropping hard. It took a mere three strokes, three times of watching her beautiful body slide up and then down again on his rigid shaft for Jordan to go mindless.

He cupped her breasts, arched his back, and exploded like a savage. To his immense surprise and pleasure, just as he began to regain sanity he heard Georgia sob and opened his eyes to watch her take her own pleasure. He was still hard, still buried deep inside her. She rocked her hips, her breasts bouncing, until she threw her head back and groaned out her second orgasm.

When she collapsed on his chest, Jordan put his arms around her and held her tight. He loved her so much it hurt, but when he decided to tell her, he heard her breathing even into the deep rhythm of sleep.

Pushing her hair from her face he studied her features. Her temples were damp from her exertions, her lips swollen and rosy, her cheeks still flushed. He kissed her forehead and the bridge of her nose. "I love you," he whispered, and though she didn't reply she did snuggle closer.

Smiling, Jordan eased her to his side so he could remove the used condom and find the blankets. It took him scant minutes and then he was back, pulling her onto his chest again, determined to keep her as close as possible. Forever.

Her heartbeat echoed in his chest, and with his mind at peace, Jordan dozed off.

GEORGIA WOKE the next morning to an empty bed. She automatically reached for Jordan, but he was gone. Then she heard him singing in his low, sexy voice, and with a smile, she climbed out of bed and wrapped the sheet around her.

His apartment was fabulous. Located over the three-car garage for the main house, it was open and spacious. The bedroom and private bath were the only doorways. The kitchen, breakfast nook and wide living room all flowed into each other. Since the bedroom door was open she could see Jordan at the kitchen sink, measuring out coffee. His broad naked back made her body feel liquid and warm. He wore only a pair of faded jeans riding low on his narrow hips, and even his bare feet looked sexy. Of course he was making coffee, and she smiled.

She'd told him she loved him.

Georgia remembered her declaration with a touch of embarrassment, but decided it didn't matter. So what that he hadn't responded in kind? She knew he cared for her, and he and his family were so wonderful....

The phone rang and as Jordan turned to answer it he caught sight of her. Immediately, he forgot about the phone and started toward her with a male determination that had her blushing. "Morning," he murmured in a suggestive way.

Oh, that sexy just-up voice! Her heart picked up

speed and a wave of warmth shook her. "Good morning."

His smile was so gentle. Combined with a mostly naked superior male body, Jordan Sommerville was very potent! Georgia cleared her throat. "Aren't you going to get the phone?"

"The answering machine will pick up."

No sooner did he say it than it happened. Georgia missed the beginning of the message because Jordan kissed her while slowly unwinding the sheet from her body. He held it out to her sides and looked at her in the bright morning sunlight cascading through the kitchen windows.

"You're so beautiful."

She thought to tease him about needing glasses, since she knew her hair was tangled and her makeup smudged, but then the person on the phone said, *"So as of a few hours ago, the bar is officially shut down. Who knows how long it'll last, but I knew you'd be happy to hear it. Serving minors is a serious offense, and about the quickest way around to lose your licence. I think we can probably keep him shut down. Anyway, give me a call when you can and I'll fill you in on the rest of the details."*

They were both frozen, Jordan in what appeared to be satisfaction, Georgia with dawning horror.

She was unemployed.

She yanked the sheet away from Jordan and held it to her chin to cover her nudity. She felt lost and vulnerable and scared. What would she do now? Good God, she couldn't make the bills without that job! In a daze, Georgia swallowed hard and turned away from Jordan.

He caught her shoulder, and his voice sounded a bit harsh. "Where are you going?"

Blankly, her mind in a muddle, she stared at him. "I have to go find a job. I have to...I don't know. I have to do something." Then, before she could stop herself, she whispered, *"Jordan, what am I going to do?"*

His expression softened, and she wondered if what she saw in his eyes was pity. Details whipped through her mind with the speed of light. Scheduled dental checkups for the kids. The premium on her mother's health insurance. The gas and electric, the mortgage.... She hadn't had a chance to save up much money yet. She'd been too busy making repairs. And now...

The sheet fell to the floor, forgotten as she covered her face with her hands, knowing she'd failed yet again. "I have to find a job." She said it once more, hoping to make herself understand. But she'd already looked everywhere before accepting the work at the bar. Nowhere else had paid enough. For a high school dropout who could only work certain hours because of being a mother, she wasn't exactly prime employment material.

Jordan's hands curved around her shoulders, caressing, comforting. "It's too early to do anything right now. I'll call the sheriff back in a bit and get all the details, okay?"

The sheriff? Not his brother, so it must have been the one who'd wanted them arrested. She'd known he was watching the bar, that he was fed up with the nightly problems that seemed to erupt....

Jordan interrupted her thoughts. "I have a few solutions, sweetheart. Will you listen to me?"

Georgia realized she'd put her worries onto him;

she'd come to depend on him whether she wanted to admit it or not. How had she let that happen?

He'd once offered to let her work for him, but that would be no more than charity and she didn't think she could stand it. She shook her head as she tried to pull away.

"You *will* listen," Jordan stated, and urged her toward his sofa.

"What is there to say? I won't work for you—"

"You don't have to." Jordan gently pushed her into the seat, then plucked up the sheet and handed it to her. Georgia wrapped it around herself; she had all but forgotten she was nude.

"Now just listen." He caught both her hands and held tight. "You said you wanted options, well here're two." He drew a deep breath. "You can marry me." He waited, watching her closely, and when she only stared at him in shock, his expression hardened. "Or you can teach dance at your own studio."

That was every bit as confusing as his proposal. Only...he hadn't really proposed. Not once had he ever said he loved her, only that he wanted her. And last night he'd admitted to respecting her, admiring her...

"Georgia, are you listening to me?"

She blinked. "Yes, but...I don't have a studio."

Jordan seemed to be getting angrier by the moment. "I found you one. It's in the center of town. It used to be a novelty shop, but the owner is retiring and the place is wide and airy and with a little renovation it'd be perfect."

She sat there, naked but for a sheet, confusion weighing her down. "A novelty shop?"

Jordan grabbed her chin and kissed her hard. He actually trembled he was so furious. "I already agreed to buy the building so you might as well agree." When she still hesitated, he barked, "You said you enjoy teaching dance, and Misty and Honey assure me there'll be—"

Incredulous, Georgia shot off the sofa to stare down at him. "You bought me a *building*?"

He didn't stand, but instead sprawled back in his seat and put his arms along the sofa back. Every single muscle in his arms and chest and shoulders was defined. "Yes."

"Ohmigod." She paced away, but had taken no more than ten steps when she whirled back around to face him. "How can you buy me a building? Nobody buys someone else a building!"

His eyes narrowed. "I also asked you to marry me."

"No." Wildly, she shook her head. "You told me I *could* marry you. It's not at all the same thing."

"You want all the fanfare? You want me to go down on one knee?"

"No!" Her head had started to pound and she felt queasy. It would be so easy to marry him, to let him fix everything, but she'd sworn she wouldn't do that again. She felt wetness on her cheeks and realized she was crying. Her heart ached and she said on a near wail, "I can't marry you, Jordan. Why would you even suggest such a thing?"

His eyes closed briefly; he rubbed a hand over his face. "You said you loved me."

"I do, but...you have everything. You have a wonderful supportive family and a great job, an education and respectability, a home and money and—"

He came to his feet so quickly, she yelped and nearly tripped over the trailing sheet. Jordan gripped her arms.

"So that's what you love about me?" he roared, scaring her half silly. "What I can give you?"

She'd never seen Jordan like this. She'd watched him easily subdue a man twice his size. She'd watched him face off with his brothers. She'd seen Jordan angry and frustrated and deliberately provoking, but she'd never seen him in this type of rage. Oddly enough, though he'd startled her, she wasn't afraid of him.

"No." She emphasized that with a tiny shake of her head. "I love you," she said very quietly, choking on her tears, "because of who you are."

He stepped up to her until she had to tip her head back to see his face, until his bare chest brushed her knuckles clutching the sheet and his feet were braced on either side of hers. He surrounded her and overwhelmed her and then he whispered, "That's why I love you, too."

More tears blurred her vision and she rubbed them away, sniffing and gulping and sounded horribly like a frog. "But I—"

"You're going to really piss me off," he informed her, "if you put yourself down again." She hiccuped on a laugh. Jordan raised one hand to gently smooth her cheek. "Weren't you listening last night, baby? I love you. I'm crazy nuts about you. My whole family knows it, even my mother. Yes I have all the things you mentioned, but I don't have you. And without you, I'm not going to be happy."

"Oh Jordan." She swallowed hard. "You really love me?"

He shook his head. "What did you think? That I just enjoy giving foot rubs?"

She lost what little control she had on her emotions and dropped the sheet again to throw herself into his arms. "I love you so much."

"I do, you know," he whispered. "Enjoy rubbing on you, I mean." She laughed as he cradled her close. He slid his hands down to her backside and lifted her. "Marry me, Georgia. Let me have you. Let me make your family my own and give you mine and we can both be happy."

"It...it doesn't feel right to take that much from you."

He rocked her into his erection. "Does this feel right?" When she nodded, he kissed her gently. "And this?"

"Jordan..."

"And this?"

Georgia had known from the start that he could seduce with just a few whispered words. Now she had firsthand proof.

———— Epilogue ————

"HEY DAD!"

Jordan looked up from making salad as Lisa came barreling through the front door, followed closely by Adam and two dogs, one a mixed-breed puppy and the other an ancient dachshund. They'd all been outside playing and smelled of sunshine and fresh crisp air. Between the children laughing and the dogs barking, the house was always filled with excitement.

Jordan knelt down and caught the children to him, hugging them fiercely. Life, he thought, was pretty damn good. "Mommy's home," Lisa told him, after a loud wet kiss to his cheek.

Seconds later Georgia strolled in. Under her coat, she wore her workout clothes of leotard and tights, guaranteed to make his blood boil. Seeing the skintight outfits affected him more strongly than her stage costumes had.

Of course, nothing affected him as much as her bare, beautiful skin.

He stood, and with the kids still close to his side and the dogs jumping between them, he gave her a long, thorough kiss. "Hi," he whispered and she smiled back.

Her smiles, he decided, were downright lethal.

"What time is everyone due to arrive?"

Jordan took her coat from her and hung it on the

back of an oak chair. Thanks to Gabe's handyman skills, the remodelled kitchen had become a favorite hangout for everyone. "You have time to shower, if that's what you're wondering."

"Can I do anything to help you first?"

Jordan went back to preparing his salad. "The sauce you made yesterday is already heating, and the spaghetti will go on as soon as the water starts to boil." He glanced at the kids. "My assistant chefs can wash their hands and start to work on the garlic bread."

Lisa grinned up at him. She'd lost another tooth and her words now whistled when she spoke. "Grandma said she's bringin' dessert."

Jordan shook his head. Grandma, he knew darn good and well, was smitten with Mr. Malone, who would also be in attendance. Ruth had moved into his vacated apartments over the garage. Neither he nor Georgia had wanted her to, but she'd insisted on giving them time to be alone. When Misty and Honey had begged her to stay close since the babies loved her so much, she'd agreed. She was now a paid housekeeper/sitter with her own measure of independence, which she loved.

She also loved the way Mr. Malone hung around on the pretense of visiting his daughters, though Sawyer and Morgan were both quite disgruntled by that situation. Jordan sympathized with them. He didn't understand the attraction at all. Ruth was so sweet and open and loving, but Mr. Malone—they'd known the man for ages and still called him mister—was so detached. Ruth claimed he was softening and that he wasn't at all detached when they were alone. He wasn't detached with any of the kids, either, and he was openly impressed with Casey.

Georgia touched his cheek. "You've got that protective look about you again."

Jordan grinned at her. "Do you know how many people will be here tonight?" When she shook her head, sidetracked just as he'd hoped, he said, "Fourteen, if we include all the kids. When you add the four of us, that's a lot of confusion. Are you sure you're up to this after working all day?"

Adam crossed his arms in the same pose Jordan used. "We'll need lots of garlic bread!"

Georgia laughed. "Yes, I'm up to it, and yes, we'll need lots of bread." Then to Jordan, "You know dancing doesn't tire me. Just the opposite, I always feel energized after a class."

In the two months since their small, quiet marriage, Georgia had gotten her studio set up and filled to the maximum with students. She taught not only dance classes for the fun of it, but also aerobics. She had people of all ages coming throughout the day. And true to her word, she was always bursting with energy.

Especially in the bedroom.

Jordan had to pull his thoughts away from that direction or he'd never survive the massive family gathering. Georgia left to shower and dress and a few minutes later all the relatives started to arrive.

He wasn't surprised to see Casey with yet another beautiful young lady. He seldom saw the same girl twice these days, and other than a few surprise meetings, Emma hadn't been around.

At her first bite of dinner, Georgia smiled at Jordan

and said, "Delicious. You really are perfect at everything, aren't you?"

Jordan grinned. He was used to her saying that, but obviously his family wasn't.

Morgan choked on his spaghetti, then doubled over laughing. "Maybe perfect for you," he laughed, "but I think old Jordan is plenty flawed. Now Malone, she prefers men with a little more steel, don't ya, sweetheart?"

Misty pretended she hadn't heard him, though everyone could see her trying not to smile. Amber said, "Daddy's nasty."

Sawyer shook his head. "Can't you control him, Misty? He gets more outrageous by the day."

"Look who's talking!" Morgan said.

Sawyer was trying to eat and love on his wife and son at the same time. His mother took Shohn so she and Brett could spoil him just a bit, and Honey found her chair bumping up against her husband's.

Gabe tipped Elizabeth's chair toward him and kissed her hard. She didn't even try to fight him off. Adam mimicked their smooching sounds until everyone laughed. Lisa announced to the table at large that her grandma and Mr. Malone were playing footsie beneath the table.

CASEY SAT BACK in his seat and watched them all with an indulgent smile. Things sure had changed over the past few years, and he loved it. He missed having Jordan so close, but they visited often, and it was obvious Jordan was as happy as a man could be. His father and uncles had all found the perfect women for them.

The girl beside Casey cleared her throat. She was

uncomfortable in the boisterous crowd, but it didn't matter. He doubted he'd see her again anyway. She was beautiful, sexy, and anxious to please him—but she wasn't perfect for him. Though he was only eighteen and had quite a bit of college ahead of him, not to mention all his other plans, Casey couldn't help but wonder if he'd ever meet the perfect mate.

An image of big brown eyes, filled with sexual curiosity, sadness, and finally rejection, formed in his mind. With a niggling dread that wouldn't ease up, Casey wondered if he'd already found the perfect girl—but had sent her away.

Then he heard Georgia talking to his date, and pulled himself out of his reverie. No, she wasn't perfect, but she didn't keep him awake nights, either. And that was good, because no matter what, no matter how he felt now, he would not let his plans get off track. He decided to forget all about women and the future and simply enjoy the night with his family.

IT WAS LATE when Casey finally got home after dropping off his date, and he'd just pulled off his shirt when a fist started pounding on the front door. He and his father met in the hall, both of them frowning. Honey pulled on her robe and hustled after them.

When Sawyer got the door open, they found themselves confronted with Emma's father. He had his daughter by the arm, and he was obviously furious.

Casey's first startled thought was that Emma wasn't gone after all. Then he got a good look at her face and he erupted in rage.

He'd been wrong. His plans would change after all. In a big way.

Some secrets are better left buried...

Yesterday's Scandal by

WILKINS

A mysterious stranger has come to town...

Former cop Mac Cordero was going undercover one last time to find and exact revenge on the man who fathered, then abandoned him. All he knew was that the man's name was McBride—a name, that is synonymous with scandal.

...and he wants her!

Responsible, reliable Sharon Henderson was drawn to the sexy-as-sin stranger. She couldn't help falling for him hard and fast. Then she discovered that their love was based on a lie....

YOU WON'T WANT TO MISS IT!

On sale September 2000 at your favorite retail outlet.

HARLEQUIN®
Makes any time special ™

**Don't miss
an exciting opportunity
to save on the purchase of
*Harlequin and Silhouette books!***

Buy any two Harlequin or
Silhouette books and save
$10.00 off future Harlequin
and Silhouette purchases

OR

buy any three
Harlequin or Silhouette books
and save **$20.00 off** future
Harlequin and Silhouette purchases.

***Watch for details
coming in October 2000!***

PHQ400

If you enjoyed what you just read,
then we've got an offer you can't resist!

Take 2 bestselling love stories FREE!

Plus get a FREE surprise gift!

Romance is just one click away!

online book **serials**

➤ *Exclusive* to our web site, get caught up in both the daily and weekly online installments of new romance stories.

➤ Try the Writing Round Robin. Contribute a chapter to a story created by our members. Plus, winners will get prizes.

romantic **travel**

➤ Want to know where the best place to kiss in New York City is, or which restaurant in Los Angeles is the most romantic? Check out our Romantic Hot Spots for the scoop.

➤ Share your travel tips and stories with us on the romantic travel message boards.

romantic reading **library**

➤ Relax as you read our collection of Romantic Poetry.

➤ Take a peek at the Top 10 Most Romantic Lines!

Visit us online at

www.eHarlequin.com
on Women.com Networks

HARLEQUIN *Super*ROMANCE®

Here's what small-town dreams are made of!

BORN IN A
SMALL TOWN

is a special 3-in-1 collection featuring

New York Times bestselling author
Debbie Macomber's brand-new *Midnight Sons*
title, *Midnight Sons and Daughters*

Judith Bowen's latest *Men of Glory* title—
The Glory Girl

Janice Kay Johnson returns to
Elk Springs, Oregon with *Patton's Daughters*
in *Promise Me Picket Fences*

Join the search for romance in three small towns
in September 2000.

Available at your favorite retail outlet.

HARLEQUIN®
Makes any time special ™